Ryker

Billionaire Blind Dates

Book 4

Toni Denise

Chapter One
Ryker

"Wanna tell me what the hell is going on?" Ryker stared down at his friend as they stood in the kitchen.

"I don't have to tell you shit." Luke backed away to leave.

Ryker grabbed his arm, pulling him back. "No. I never said you did, but you're clearly deep into some shit and I can't fucking help if you don't tell me what's going on."

"No one asked you to play the big brother." Luke shrugged Ryker's arm off. "There's nothing going on for you to worry about. Leave me alone."

Ryker let him go this time, watching as he did. Luke was definitely up to something and, if he didn't miss his guess, was in some kind of trouble. The normally happy-go-lucky member of their friend group had been pissy for weeks. This was the first poker night he'd shown up to in a while.

"You good?" Jake asked, getting a beer from the fridge.

"Yeah," Ryker answered, trying to shake off the issues with Luke.

"Not upset it's finally your turn?" Jake joked.

Ryker sighed. "Fuck. I forgot about that."

"Not sure how you could forget something so life changing."

They both headed back to the table where the poker game was about to start and took their seats.

Ryker wasn't sure how he'd forgotten, either. It wasn't like him to forget anything, much less something like this bullshit plan they had come up with.

Of his friend group, Ryker would be the fourth to go on a series of blind dates that were set up by his friends. The catch was that these were all at a restaurant that Evan's girlfriend own, and he was a not so silent partner in, where the dates were done in the dark.

"Ryker said he forgot it was his turn," Jake announced.

"Shut up." He took a swig of his beer.

"Well, it's been successful so far, so maybe you're just scared it will work?" Evan laughed as he started to deal the cards.

It had been. Jake, Evan, and Cade had all found their significant others through this scheme they had jokingly concocted. It wasn't fear of finding someone that worried Ryker though, it was the fear of who they might set him up with, namely Catherine, Cade's sister.

Luke shook his blonde hair. "Ryker won't find anyone. That's why I was glad to go last. He has no desire to settle down."

Ryker didn't acknowledge him, instead focusing on the shit hand he'd just been dealt. The more he was around all these happy couples in his friend group, the more he wondered what it would be like to have someone that was always in your corner. Then he'd remember that the women he knew were either after his money or wanted him to play the part of the bad boy.

Tattoos showed wherever he went and he did little to dissuade anyone from thinking he was an asshole, but generally, he wasn't. The things that some women had asked him to do had blown even his mind. It wasn't what he wanted in a relationship.

"Can we focus on the game?" Ryker grunted out.

"Can I tell Kayla to send the questionnaire over?" Evan prodded.

"Whatever," he bit out. "Just play the damn game."

Ryker

Evan smiled. "As usual, Luke, you need to pick someone for him to date first."

Ryker held in a groan. That was sure to be more of a disaster than everyone else's experiences with Luke's dates. He always picked women that were exactly what everyone was avoiding. One woman practically chased Jake out of the restaurant, upset the night didn't end in a billionaire's bed.

"I'll send the information to Kayla. Been waiting on this one," Luke grinned.

"Okay. That's settled. Can we play the fucking game?" Ryker said.

Everyone laughed, but the game did get started. Each of the five of them were billionaires in their own right, all with different companies, but they played poker for change. Usually the pot at the end of the night was less than fifty bucks, but it was a way for them to get together and the low stakes meant there was no pressure here.

This was one of the few that Ryker had hosted in his place. He didn't normally like people at his place, friends or not. Things were changing though and as one of the remaining single men with only Luke for company there, they had asked him to host. He had stocked the fridge and agreed without hesitation.

Ryker loved all the women that his friends had found. They were all perfect couples, which was absolutely nauseating, but he was starting to envy it. The one person he wanted in his future was the one person he would never let in, Catherine.

She was raised in this world and deserved so much better than him. He had earned a reputation as a shrewd businessman and it was well deserved. While he wasn't the bad boy, the women thought he was. He was every inch the man that other businesses feared, for good reason.

Ryker wasn't above blackmail to get what he wanted in a business transaction. The men he dealt with left so many options open to take it, too. He had one man dedicated to researching, not just the skeletons in any company he was about to takeover, but also that of the people that were pulling the strings. It made things simpler when he was ready to make a deal.

Sometimes those men would try to retaliate against Cade before they saw reason. More than once that had meant someone had attempted to put a hit on him, unsuccessful, but no less attempted.

Ryker was used to dealing with the seedier side of things in business and Catherine didn't need to be mixed up in that. No, she deserved someone that was born and bred into her world and would fit neatly with her image. Not to mention she was in public relations, where image was everything.

"What do you think?" Cade asked.

Ryker wracked his brain and tried to find bits of the conversation he had missed with no luck. "About?"

Cade shook his head. "About the new deal that Jake is working on?"

Oh, that he already knew about. "I already told him. I don't think it's a good idea. That company is going to come with some pretty serious bullshit that you'll have to clean up."

"Would you take it?" Jake asked.

"For me? Maybe. I'd at least consider it," Ryker admitted. He rubbed a hand over his short hair and tried to focus back on the conversation. "That company is connected pretty deep with the mob, from what I could find. I don't know for sure I'd even bother with it. You'll have a tough time keeping people in line there and legal."

"Hmm," Jake scratched his chin as he thought about it. "You don't think all the numbers are legal?"

"No. I told you the numbers don't add up. They have to be padding the books." Ryker was positive of that.

"Can you get Hacker Guy to do some digging?" Jake asked.

"At least you asked," Ryker shook his head. "I'll have him run what he can on it."

Hacker Guy was actually just Matt, an employee that Ryker had that was really good at finding things people wanted to stay hidden. He was Ryker's go-to guy for things like this. His friends had grown used to helping themselves to his expertise and Catherine had started calling him Hacker Guy or Hacker Man and it had stuck amongst them.

"Oh, so if I ask first, I can put him on my payroll?" Evan teased.

"No, but if you ask first, I might let him do some work for you," Ryker answered. "Except Cade." He glared at his friend.

"Whatever. We all know he will help us with or without your permission." Cade glared back.

Cade had used his employee for months to track his father while he was threatening Cade and Catherine. The problem was that he hadn't told any of them that this was going on even when the threats became real and started impacting the restaurant. His father was in jail now though, and hopefully that was the end of things.

"So I shouldn't tell you that I already have him looking for my missing siblings?" Cade shrugged.

One thing that Cade's father had revealed throughout his chaotic run of threats and destruction was that he had two other children that he could use to do his bidding if Cade wasn't willing. Cade and Catherine both were unaware until that moment.

"Jokes on you. Your sister already asked for permission because she can follow instructions, unlike some people. But if it makes you feel better to think you are getting one over on me, then feel free," Ryker quipped.

Cade grunted and crossed his arms, clearly unaware that his sister had told Ryker what they were doing. "Whatever."

The rest of the night was much lighter conversations and joking. Luke was still stoic compared to his normal self and didn't speak much. He didn't joke at all and was the first one out the door when the night started wrapping up.

"Is he okay?" Evan asked, referring to Luke.

"I don't know. He isn't talking," Ryker admitted.

"Well, we can all help keep an eye on him, but it might be useful to have your guy dig in on what he's been up to, since it could affect everyone."

Ryker nodded. He'd already thought about it.

"Have a good night, man," Evan said as he left.

With the last one gone, Cade locked the door and turned off the outside lights. Something about having it off made him feel like no one would knock on it again. It wasn't always the case, but it made him feel better.

As he walked to his room, he contemplated Luke's problem and what it could be. Too many scenarios existed from a pregnant date to the mob. He would have Hacker Guy get on it first thing in the morning.

Chapter Two
Catherine

"You can't buy that house." Cade slammed the paperwork on the table.

"I wasn't asking you," Catherine said with a smile. Her brother was always in her business and living with him since her parents had held her and Cade's girlfriend, April, hostage in her apartment. She couldn't go back in there and didn't even want to. It had taken forever to find a place though, and now that she had, her brother was being his overbearing self about it.

"I've already bought it. The deal is done, money transferred, so it doesn't really matter what you have to say. It's a safe area and other than the real estate agent saying the neighbor is kind of a jerk, it's a great place."

Cade snorted. "Don't you want security, a doorman, something?"

"To what extent? I had one before and that didn't stop what happened, did it?" She snapped.

"Fair enough, but it's not a good idea for that house in particular. Just maybe look into that neighbor?" Cade said.

Catherine squinted at him, trying to see what he wasn't telling her. "What do you know?"

"That you should have done your research."

"Well, you can gloat about it now. Who is the neighbor?" She hated that he had her curious, and he was definitely going to gloat.

He stared her down as though debating if he was going to answer. "Nah, I think I will let you figure this one out all by your big girl self."

"Dammit Cade, just tell me."

"Little sister, I think I've changed my mind. It's a good idea. Go for it. Happy for you." With that, he rushed out of her office and left her sitting there.

"What the hell was that?" Catherine asked the empty room.

Not above looking up the information, she quickly messaged her real estate agent.

> Catherine: Hey. I know you said the neighbor is a bit of a jerk at this place, right?

> Amy: That's the rumor.

> Catherine: Who is it?

> Amy: What do you mean?

> Catherine: What's his name?

> Amy: Ryker something. He's hot as hell, but apparently an asshole. Why?

"Shit," Catherine looked away from her phone and took a deep breath before writing her back.

> Catherine: My brother knows him. Said something about looking at who my neighbor was.

> Amy: I mean, we can't change it now, but you can list it for sale again if you need to.

> Catherine: It's totally fine, nothing like that. My brother was just being an ass.

Ryker

She set her phone down and looked out the window at the rain coming down. It was beginning to seem like the day was suiting her new mood. Ryker as a neighbor of all people.

For years she had lusted after him with zero reciprocation on his part, save for one kiss that he quickly called a mistake. She didn't think it was the whole friend's sister part that was the issue either, because she'd heard from her friends that Cade had pretty much told Ryker to go for it.

Ryker wasn't uninterested, either. She caught him paying attention to her enough to get her hopes up for a while, but again, nothing. So she'd decided to put him from her mind and she was going to just move on. She had given up chasing him and hinting at anything between them just to be rejected.

Now, she was going to be neighbors with him. This should be a blast. Definitely not the best way to get him off her mind.

Maybe it was time to truly move on, do something completely different. Grabbing her phone again, she texted one of her best friends, Kayla.

Catherine: You've been telling me to sign up for months. Are you trying to talk me out of it?

Kayla: Of course not. But I am trying to be a good friend and figure out where this is coming from.

Catherine: My new neighbor.

Kayla: Oh? Did you meet them already? I thought you got your keys tonight?

Catherine: It's Ryker.

Kayla: Shut up!

Catherine: Just found out. I need a drink.

Kayla: I'll send the details over for the dates.

Catherine: Thanks.

She set her phone down on her desk again and sighed. This wasn't what she had planned for her new place. With any luck, she just wouldn't see him around, anyway. She didn't know what hours Ryker kept, but something told her he was out more than he was home.

"Hey boss, I'm going to head out unless you need anything else?" Jack, her assistant, poked his head into her office.

"I told you there was no need for you to come in on a Saturday," she reminded him.

"And yet here we are, both of us working on a weekend." He smiled at her and left.

Until her recent personal PR disaster, she hadn't bothered to have an assistant. Now, she needed one just to field the calls from reporters that were still coming months after her parents were arrested. But it seemed that Jack was determined to make her feel bad for working long hours, in addition to answering calls for her.

Taking it for the sign that it was, Catherine gathered her things and let herself out as well. It was weird doing her job halfway lately, since her own PR mess wasn't good for helping anyone else. She had to sit back and only plan. She was giving it a few more weeks and then she was going back in again in front of the cameras and anyone that questioned her personal life would just be removed from any conferences.

Catherine waited for the valet to bring her car around in the comfort of the lobby. She wasn't above using a little of her own power to not stand in the rain. Normally, she parked her own car on the private parking deck with Cade because she could. When it was nasty out, she didn't bother, someone else could do it.

If she had thought it all the way through, she would have arranged for a car instead of driving herself, but she wanted to buy this house completely on her own. Her brain this morning convinced her that also meant driving herself there. It made no sense, but here she was.

When her car was pulled around, she quickly got in and headed for her new house. Amy would be meeting her there with the keys and she was ready to take ownership and get all the new things she'd bought delivered and setup. Taking it one step further, she'd even taken vacation time for next week.

She'd be working, of course, but not in the office. Jack would no doubt give her heavy sighs as she did. She tried to convince him to also take time off, but he declined. His boyfriend couldn't take the time off too, so they were waiting to take a vacation together.

Catherine admitted she was a bit jealous of all the couples around her now. She wanted that. Wanted someone to come home to and to share everything with. Maybe a reason to not want to work all the time.

One problem with that scenario was her crush, or whatever it was, on Ryker. She had wasted a good amount of time pining after him instead of someone that maybe wanted her back. The other issue was that she scared a lot of men away with her direct and firm demeanor.

Catherine could play the game as well as anyone, but given the opportunity, she preferred being the one in charge of everything because then you knew it would go right. Cade and his friends challenged her often and weren't put off by the power she held. Once, though, she went out with a man who told her a woman's job was to bow to her husband and he would have to train her. Gross and absolutely not.

She pulled up in front of her new home and settled in to wait for Amy. She was about twenty minutes early. If it wasn't for the rain, she would get out and walk around Ryker be damned. Now she was trapped in her car, looking at the rain fall on her car and the beautiful brownstone she was now the proud owner of.

Her phone chimed, pulling her out of her peaceful thoughts. Catherine pulled it out of her bag and unlocked it, opening the message from Amy.

> Amy: Hey! Hope you haven't left yet. There's an accident and everything is backed up. I don't know how long I'll be.

> Catherine: I'm here already, actually. No problem though, you can't control the traffic.

> Amy: I'm so sorry. If you want to leave, I can call you when I'm close.

> Catherine: I'll let you know if I leave. Just going to hang out here for now.

> Amy: Okay. Sorry again.

Catherine screamed at the tapping on her window and her phone went flying as she panicked.

Chapter Three
Catherine

"What the hell, Catherine?" Ryker's gruff voice, muffled through her closed windows, shouted.

Pressing a hand to her racing heart, she took a deep breath before rolling the window down. "What the hell me? What the hell you? You just scared the crap out of me."

"Why are you parked outside my house?" he demanded.

This was going to be fun. It seemed Cade had failed to inform his friend that she was his new neighbor. "I live here."

"No you don't. I do."

Catherine rolled her eyes. "Not with you. I bought this house. I'm waiting on my realtor with the keys."

Ryker swore and she couldn't help the small grin that creeped out at getting to surprise him. She had convinced herself that he already knew.

"Anyway, you can go," she told him.

"Where's your agent?" he asked.

"Stuck in traffic," Catherine answered.

A look of defeat crossed his face. "Come on then," he said, waving his arm for her to get out.

"What?" she sputtered.

"If she's in the mess that is out there, she won't be here for a while. You can wait at my place until she gets here."

Confused at this random act of kindness from Ryker, Catherine didn't move.

"Come on," he said, sounding annoyed.

Not prepared to argue this offer, Catherine quickly looked for her phone, finding it in the passenger seat before rolling her window up, turning the car off, and opening the door. Immediately, Ryker was there, offering her his hand.

She took it, once again surprised by him as he took off at a brisk pace towards his home. They rushed through the rain before finally reaching his porch and both standing under the small roof as he unlocked the door.

"Why did you buy that house?" he asked as they walked into his home.

"I liked the home. I didn't want to live in my apartment anymore and I've been staying at Cade's, but I wasn't going to do that forever. This one came up for sale and I bought it."

"You just had to live next to me?" Ryker shrugged out of his coat and hung it on a rack by the door.

"I didn't know you were the neighbor until today. Cade didn't know the address of this property until today and then he refused to tell me who my neighbor was, so I had to ask Amy and only just found out."

"Cade could have called me," Ryker muttered.

"He could have, but he's also an ass, so..." Catherine let it trail off.

Ryker grunted his agreement. "Coffee?" he asked.

"Anything warm would be great," she answered, following him through to a massive kitchen,

"I really didn't know you lived here. I just assumed you were in a penthouse or basement or something," she half-joked.

"It is what it is," he told her, putting the coffee pod in the machine.

Chill Ryker wasn't someone she was used to. Catherine stood awkwardly in the kitchen and waited in silence for the coffee to brew. She studied him as he moved around his kitchen and wondered what was going through his mind.

"Cream and sugar?" he asked.

She nodded.

He pulled both out and set them on the counter. "You can have a seat."

She walked around the bar and slid onto one of the stools. "Are you okay?" she asked after a minute.

"Yeah," he ground out.

"You know I wasn't going to bother you, right? I can go sit in my car, honestly." She was going to get that warm cup of coffee first, though.

"It's fine." He put the cup in front of her and went back to make another.

"Ryker, it's obviously not fine. I swear I didn't know that we were going to be neighbors, but I doubt we will see each other much. I'll just drink this coffee quickly and you can have your space back." Catherine poured the cream into her cup and added a bit of sugar before giving it a stir. It was piping hot, but she was prepared to guzzle it just to get out of here right now.

"You're fine. There's no need to wait in your car. You can wait here because it's going to be a while before you have keys to next door."

"I know that you like your personal space, Ryker. I'm not trying to be in your way."

"I never said that you were."

"You're acting like it. Frankly, I'm confused you invited me in at all. It's like you're scared to be anywhere near me most of the time." There, she'd said what she was thinking.

"I have a lot on my mind right now, Cat. I am not going to do this with you and you aren't going to go wait in the cold for hours, either. Make yourself at home."

Cade jerked his coffee from the machine so fast it splashed on his hand. As he swore, Catherine was out of her seat, already looking at his hand.

"I'm fine," he told her, pulling his hand back.

"Fine. Sorry for being concerned," she spit back at him.

"Dammit," Ryker whispered. "Why isn't anything with you easy?"

"What is that supposed to mean?" She stiffened her spine, prepared to go to battle with him over it.

"Nothing. I'm going to my office. Living room is through there and the remotes are on the table."

With that, Ryker left her standing there alone in his kitchen. He didn't even take his own cup with him, just stormed out instead.

Catherine huffed and went back to her coffee. It wasn't like she asked him to let her in. She was perfectly fine to wait in her car like she had planned on. It wasn't cold in her car with the heat on, anyway.

Something stopped her from storming back out, though. Maybe it was the fact that she was standing in his sanctuary. The one place she knew he didn't like people to be. He didn't want anyone in his space and that included his friends. He rarely hosted their poker nights, preferring to go to someone else's home instead.

Ryker was an enigma of a man. Hot one minute, cold the next. A bit like the October weather they were having at the moment.

With nothing else to do, she let herself into his living room and took a seat, carefully placing the still very hot coffee on the table. The overstuffed black leather furniture wasn't a surprise and suited the man she knew. The pops of color in this room, those were. The yellow accent pillows threw her off right away.

He did have a pleasant garden out back and a beautiful view of it from where she sat. Rather than turn the TV on, Catherine sat and watched the raindrops chase each other down the window. Her mind wandered as she did and as much as she didn't want it to be to Ryker, he was all she could think about as she sat there in his home.

She wondered what was going on with him being so welcoming in the beginning and then what he might be up to. It was likely that he was just busy. Ryker being short with her, or anyone for that matter, wasn't strange. Being concerned and fixing her a cup of coffee that was weird.

She reached for it and took a hesitant sip, finding it a pleasant temperature. Any other day she would have turned down coffee this late in the day, but today it seemed fitting. It was nasty outside, and she was still a little cold.

"Couldn't figure out how to work it?" he asked.

She turned to find him standing in the doorway. "I didn't even try. I was just watching the rain. It's so peaceful."

"I thought you just sprinkled tidbits of chaos everywhere you want. It's nice to know you like calm sometimes," he was joking, but she still took offense.

Catherine sat up again, no longer relaxed. "Yeah. I should probably call Amy."

"Traffic app says everything is at a stand-still," Ryker told her.

Damn. "Well, I guess I should tell her to try again tomorrow then, and I should make my way back to Cade's for the night."

"Were you planning to stay over there tonight? It's not furnished, is it?"

"I have an air mattress in my car. I was just going to order pizza and celebrate owning my own place." She stood, uncomfortable that she had admitted anything to him.

"Didn't you own the apartment?" he asked.

Oh, so now the man wanted to have an actual conversation? "Kind of. I owned it, but my father helped me buy it. It was messy and just not something I did on my own. This house is mine. I own it, I made the decisions, I paid for it."

Ryker nodded. "Well, I don't think you're going to get back to Cade's, either."

It couldn't be that she was stuck. "Let me check the app."

It didn't take long to pull it up and see that she wasn't going to make it there either. At this point, she was going to need a hotel or sit in traffic for hours.

"You can stay in the guest room," he announced.

She couldn't have closed her mouth if she tried. Her jaw hung open at the mere fact that Cade was allowing her in his space and then offering her a place to sleep. He literally had done his best not to be anywhere near her in months, and now this?

"I can get a hotel," she assured him.

"And waste money. It's fine, just stay here." He walked out of the room like everything was decided.

Catherine followed him. "Not to look a gift horse in the mouth, but why would you let me?" She called after him.

"You hungry?" he asked instead of answering.

She was, actually. "Yes."

Taking a seat at the bar again, she watched Ryker seemingly in his element as he pulled ingredients out and lined them up on the counter. A pot came out next before he turned to face her.

"Pasta Carbonara okay?"

"You... cook?" she barely got out over her surprise.

"I didn't grow up rich, remember? If you wanted to eat, you had to learn to cook something with a few ingredients. I admit this is a step up from buttered noodles, and definitely higher end ingredients, but I assure you, it isn't hard."

That was probably the most he'd ever said at one time to her. "Umm, yeah, that sounds great."

"Okay," he said before putting his back to her again.

Ryker made quick work of cooking the dish. She'd had it before, but not watched someone make it. Her eyes were glued to his hands, watching him move from pot to pot as he cooked and stirred.

"Here," he said, handing her a plate.

"Thanks," she croaked out.

"Don't turn this into something, Cat," he warned.

"Like what?" He had this uncanny ability to ruin any sense of relaxation she had.

"I just am offering you a place to stay and making sure you're fed. That's all it is."

She nodded. No chance was she going to take his nice demeanor personally. Hell, she was more confused than anything.

"I'll show you the room when you're done and then go get your bag out of the car if you give me your keys." He took a big bite of his own pasta from where he stood, leaning on the counter, as far away from her as possible in this room.

"I can get it. I need to get my computer and stuff, too. Plus, I still need to call Amy." She'd completely forgotten about her.

"I'll get it. It's getting dark already, and it's still nasty out." The words were an offer, but the tone left no room to say no.

"Fine," she relented and explained what bags she needed.

Twenty minutes later, she had settled in a guest room and Ryker was bringing her things up to her.

Chapter Four
Ryker

Ryker studied his new neighbor as she did yoga in her new backyard. He wasn't being creepy. It was more that it was impossible not to look. From his bedroom window, where he stood most mornings and stared out into his yard, he had a perfect view of her.

It had been a week since she stayed the night in his spare bedroom, and he couldn't shake the urge to go talk to her. He hadn't. He wouldn't. But the urge was ever present.

He blinked a few times, pushing the side of her from his mind as he walked away from the window. This routine of his would need to change, or at the very least, move to the first floor.

Back to the matter at hand. He needed to focus on Luke. The kid was still not returning his calls, and Ryker was starting to get genuinely pissed at him. It was one thing to not want to share, but another if you are actively avoiding someone. It only means that you know you're up to no good.

His research had led him nowhere, though. Luke's portfolio didn't appear to be in any trouble, both at surface level and deeper.

Ryker

Luke didn't appear to have any new habits or acquaintances that Ryker could figure out. All in all, he'd hit a dead end.

His doorbell rang as he left his bedroom and Ryker came down the stairs with a heavy sigh. He didn't need or want company right now, and everyone should know that. It was probably Catherine. She hadn't bothered him once, but he could see her becoming a nuisance.

Ryker didn't bother to look out the peephole, pulling the door open instead. "What?" he demanded of the newcomer.

"I have a delivery for you," said the man.

Taking him in, he appeared like he was in his late teens, wearing jeans and a sweatshirt, holding a large manilla envelope.

"Ryker?"

He nodded.

"You've been served." He shoved the envelope at him. "Have a good day."

"What the fuck?" Ryker asked out loud as he closed the door back.

He carried the envelope to the counter and pulled out the paperwork from within. It appeared he was being sued, not for the first time. Ryker shrugged and thumbed the paperwork, looking for who had the nerve to sue him and why.

"What the actual fuck?" he asked again.

The paperwork indicated that some woman whose name he didn't even recognize was suing him for child support after an apparent encounter between them had led to the little one not named in this paperwork.

Ryker took a photo and sent it over to his lawyer. This needed to be handled because he was absolutely positive that he hadn't fathered a child. One thing he was always sure to do was wrap it up, and he knew at least the first name of every woman he ever slept with. At least, he thought he did.

Dropping into his sofa, he rubbed circles on his temples as he stressed over the papers that were now on the coffee table in front of him. This had to be a sick joke. He didn't mess around in business,

21

and he damn sure didn't mess around with this shit in his personal life. He needed to find her and figure out what the fuck was going on.

> Ryker: I need everything you can find on Danielle Wadson.

> Matt (Hacker Guy): Good morning, boss. It's Saturday, take time off.

> Ryker: This is personal and I need it yesterday.

> Matt: Fine.

> Ryker: Everything.

Angry and annoyed, Ryker rose to his feet again and began pacing. So much for Luke's problems. It looks like he now had his own.

His doorbell rang once again and Ryker stormed to the door, prepared to go off on the same kid from before. Just as he did, he saw Catherine standing there instead.

"What?" he snapped at her.

"I brought you some breakfast to repay your kindness from next week," Catherine smiled as she spoke. "Clearly I didn't need to worry about that, since you're back to being a jerk again."

Ryker leaned on the door as he looked at her. "Dammit Cat. Just come in."

"I can just set this on the counter and get out of your way," she assured him, holding the plate up.

"What is it?" he questioned.

"Cinnamon rolls. I made them this morning."

He squinted at her in mistrust. "From a can?"

"From flour," she answered, not seeming annoyed at his question.

"Really?" Ryker pressed on, unable to believe it.

She nodded. "I don't bake often, but I do know how and if you tell anyone, I will deny it."

Ryker threw his head back in open laughter. "I won't ruin your image. Are you sure you aren't poisoning me and trying to take this house instead? I won't leave it to you in my will."

A smile finally appeared. "No? Damn. Who are you leaving it to? Sounds like I need to get to know someone fast."

"Luke." First name that came to mind.

Catherine did the most unladylike thing he'd seen her do. She snorted. "I'll pass on the house then. I guess you can survive if my options are you or Luke."

Ryker's phone rang, and he pulled it out to see his lawyer calling. "Sorry. I have to take this one. I'll be just a minute."

"Have you found anything out?" Ryker demanded.

"It looks like they just filed the case this week. We are looking into the validity already and just needed to clarify that you are sure that you don't know this woman?"

"I have never heard of her. No idea where this is coming from," Ryker couldn't help his raised voice. He didn't like feeling like he was being accused of anything. "I'm paying you to figure this out, not to question me."

"Understood, but the question did need to be asked. I will have our investigators on her and I am sending a reply to her lawyer now."

"Great. Call me when it's something that makes sense." Ryker ended the call and wandered back down the hall to find Cat.

He expected her to be in the kitchen waiting for him, but she wasn't. He ambled on through to his living room to find her with his paperwork in one hand, her other hand running through her bobbed hair.

"That's private," Ryker demanded.

Catherine jumped but didn't put the paperwork down. "I can see that. Give me a moment," she held up one manicured nail in his direction.

Was she serious? Like he was just going to wait for her to finish prying? "I'm not kidding. Put it down and keep your mouth shut about it."

She looked up from her reading and rolled her eyes at him. "Why is she doing this?" she asked.

"For child support," he answered dryly.

Catherine bit her lip for a moment and then looked him in the eyes. "Do you know her?"

"No," he clipped.

"Then what is the purpose behind this?" she asked.

"I don't fucking know," he admitted. "And now that you know about it, you better keep the information to yourself or I don't care who the hell you are. I will sue you."

She waved a hand at him dismissively. "Who would I even tell? But if it makes you feel better, I can pinky swear not to tell anyone."

"You're starting to piss me off," he warned.

"Only starting? Must be losing my touch." Catherine walked from the room.

"Where are you going?" He followed.

"I need my phone," she told him. "Taking these with me so you don't lock me out. I'll be right back."

Ryker lunged forward, pulled at the papers in her hand.

Catherine merely stepped to the side as though this was expected. "I have a brother," she reminded him.

Ryker took two deep breaths.

"If I leave these here, will you let me back in?" she bargained.

"Won't even lock the door, scout's honor," Ryker told her.

"Scout? Right." She turned to leave again. "I'll be right back."

He was curious enough to see what she had to say. He'd wait for her to come back, but he wasn't going to let her take photos of these documents. It would take only one to leak and it would create a mess for him.

Like the ball of energy that she always was, Catherine burst back through his front door. Her laptop was balanced with one arm on her hip as she waved her phone in the air. "Found it," she smiled.

Ryker took another breath. "What did you need it here for?"

"To show you something. I have a great memory and I just need to confirm it before I tell you."

"What?"

"One second." she held up a finger.

More annoyed, Ryker did his best to wait her out. It was typically worth it with her, but he wasn't sure he was going to make it.

"Ah ha!" she shouted. "Look. So if this kid is yours, based on how old they are, assuming this was filed recently and the math is correct, you were a little occupied."

Catherine held up her phone for him to see. It was photos of him and Jake in South America where they had gone for six weeks when they nearly lost a deal that they were going in together on. It had been tense, and they had pushed their dates out several times.

"Unless she can prove she went with you on that trip, I'd say you're in the clear even before a DNA test. Seems odd that she would try this because a simple test would solve this problem and honestly, you could just pay the expedite fee and have it back super quick."

Catherine was in her element to fix things. He didn't ask for her help, hadn't planned on telling anyone about this at all, but here she was already jumping in. He couldn't take his eyes off her.

"Sorry," she said, catching on to him watching her. "I didn't go through anything at first. It was just sitting there face up and I couldn't help it." She shrugged, but her face had gone red, clearly a little embarrassed.

"I got served them this morning. You're right, I don't understand the angle here either." Ryker took a seat, not waiting for Catherine to first.

"I know you didn't ask for my help, but you're getting it, anyway. It can be repayment for that one time you let me use the guest room."

Ryker nodded. She was going to be involved now. He knew that about her and telling her to butt out was only going to lead to an argument, that she'd win when he got tired of arguing with her. "Fine."

"Ah, there's the Ryker we know and love," she teased at his rough tone. "Is there a deal you're working on that could be messed up or delayed by this?"

"Nothing I'm even thinking of doing would be impacted," he answered. "Best she could hope for would be a month of child support while we waited for test results."

Catherine looked at her phone, her nails tapping the screen with her finger, filling the silence. "That's a long shot. I mean, the amount you'd be ordered to pay would be more than some people would make in a year, but why bother when she'd just have to pay it back? Odds are she couldn't even spend it fast enough before the results came back, and you'd just get it back. No. I think it's something more personal."

"Personal how?" He wasn't following.

"Like someone wants to make you look bad, even if just for a little while. This is one of those things that the media would latch on to and people would follow, most not remembering it wasn't you. Those people don't matter, of course, not in the long run of what you do, but it would stick."

"Shit," he swore. "You're hired."

Catherine threw her head back as she laughed, her hair swinging as she did. "Silly man, did you think I wasn't already?"

Chapter Five
Catherine

"Send me a copy of these and whatever Hacker Guy digs up on her. I've got some things to do tonight, but I'll work on it until then," Catherine told him.

"Done. I'll just tell him to cc you on everything," he answered.

"One more thing." Catherine bit her lip, unsure of how he was going to take it. "I'll have to loop in someone from my firm to handle any public facing comments. I don't want my mess to warp what's going on and ruin whatever we are doing."

"No." Ryker stood. "No one else. Don't tell your brother, your friends, no one."

"She's great. I promise it won't be an issue and that's what NDAs are for, anyway. I've been training her myself," she explained, hoping he'd see reason even though she knew this was going to be a battle.

"I'm hiring you, and you alone. This goes nowhere else. Besides, hopefully, my lawyers can have this settled before anyone figures it out." Ryker paced. Clearly, he didn't have as much faith in his lawyers as he was trying to convince her he did. He was a stressed out man.

She decided to table the discussion for now. They could cross that bridge if and when they came to it. "I need one thing from you, an honest answer."

"Cat, you just said yourself there's no way the baby could be mine. It isn't." His tone was gruff but there were undertones of hurt there.

"That's not it. Also, it's likely impossible. The trip gives you bargaining information and enough that maybe a judge wouldn't order child support without the test. That wasn't my question, though. I wanted to know if you know her, from anywhere at all?"

Ryker looked at her like she'd sprouted a second head. "I don't know that name at all. I've never heard it before, that much I am certain of. I don't go out and get blackout drunk or fuck random chicks that I don't even know who they are. We leave that to Luke."

She rolled her eyes. "I wasn't saying you did. But she could have given you a fake name. Did you recognize her face?" Catherine pressed.

"I didn't see her face. It wasn't her that delivered this shit." He waved his hands at the papers.

Catherine didn't bother explaining that he should have looked the woman up and seen her. It was an important detail, one he'd have when the deep dive was done, but it mattered too much to wait.

She unlocked her phone once again and searched for the woman's name. The first social media profile that came up was a picture of a woman holding a baby, posted just a few days ago. Turning it around to show Ryker, she waited for him to answer her question now.

He studied the photo, but she knew the answer before he gave it. There was no hint of recognition in his eyes.

"No. I have never seen her before that I'm aware of," he confirmed.

Catherine nodded and locked her phone back. "Let me know if you hear anything else at all. Even if you don't want to tell me, Ryker. I can't help you without the details."

He nodded. "Consider it done."

She smiled, believing he would do it. "Then have a good one. I'll be around most of the day, but I have a date tonight at Kayla's restaurant, so I won't have my phone on me then, but I'll write you back after I leave."

Ryker tensed. "What do you know about this person?"

"Don't. I only told you when I would be unavailable. I'm not going to discuss it any further and you aren't going to harass Kayla for information or have Hacker Guy get it. It's a blind date, in a controlled environment." She stuck one finger out and poked him in the chest. "Butt out."

What she expected was for him to raise his palms in surrender, but that was far from what she got. Ryker took another step closer to her, causing her to need to step back or have him in her personal space.

"Consider this my friendly duty. A favor for a favor. I want to know how this date goes and what was said by this guy," he demanded.

Shocked, it took her a second to form a reply. "No. That's not how this works."

"It's how it's going to work," he answered smugly.

He thought he was going to demand information from her? Not. "Then do your own PR work, Ryker. I don't need another brother, one is enough. This is a place owned by your friend, where all but two of you have done dates at. I am not going to come over here and gossip about anything or have you vet anyone. I know how to do my own investigation if I need it, and who to call."

Ryker's nostrils flared as he worked to control his temper at being told no. "Fine," he ground out. "But you tell me immediately if there are any red flags."

She wanted to tell him to butt out again, but since she didn't expect any issues, she could concede this point. "Fine. If things get weird, I will let you know."

He gave her a curt nod.

"I'll see you later. Have a good rest of your day and send me everything. Don't forget."

"Let me know what you think when he sends over the investigation," he told her.

She almost smiled. Did he think she was going to hold back her opinion? Working with Ryker was going to be interesting, a push and shove for power and she was looking forward to it. "Of course," she said simply.

He walked her out and waited on his porch as she walked to her own home. She didn't turn back and look at him again, but she could feel his eyes on her. Too much time in his company was going to make her wish for things she couldn't have again.

Catherine curled up on her sofa and considered her date tonight. The man wouldn't be able to see her, but she still needed to pick out her outfit. He would not get a chance to see her today either, not after declining the option to chat with her before the date.

In her mind, she'd decided on a rule that there needed to be three dates before she would be willing to meet someone in person, and they needed to chat with her, build the relationship. This guy could open the chat after this date and she'd just call him cautious, but if he didn't, she wasn't going on a second date.

Her thoughts wandered back to her neighbor, though. Seeing a protectiveness in him she hadn't seen since the day her parents had been arrested. Ryker had scooped her up then, holding her tight to him as everything unfolded with the arrests.

She wouldn't normally have let him, not just because of their own history, but because she was strong and didn't want people to think otherwise. At that time, she'd fallen apart and let him hold her while she did. It was understandable, a completely normal reaction to the shit that happened to her. What wasn't normal was the way Ryker had soothed her.

Ryker had held her close and told her everything would be fine. His voice, his actions, were just so caring that she couldn't let him go. She needed support, and he was there.

And then it had been over. Ryker had checked on her when he'd come by Cade's house in the first few weeks and then they'd gone back to strangers. The about face he pulled had her head spinning. Before the incident, she'd decided to let Ryker go as a crush, but when he'd gone back to cold and distant, she knew it was time. It only helped to solidify her resolve.

Her body had other plans when she saw him, though. The man was hotter than should be legal, and tattoos only enhanced him. On no one else had she found a full sleeve of tattoos sexy, but on him, perfection.

"Stop," she told herself, needing to get her thoughts away from that path.

Catherine opened the dating app again to double check the time for tonight's date and see if he had accepted her invitation to chat. Sadly, the date was still at six, but no chat option was there.

She was going to make tonight an enjoyable experience, anyway. Maybe this guy had terrible experiences in the past and wanted to chat in person first. No need to judge right away, right? It was hard not to, though.

Several hours to go before the date, Catherine grabbed a book off her shelf and got comfortable. Distracting herself from her real-world problems by focusing on some fictional ones was her favorite way to unwind. It also helped that she knew all these romance books would have a happy ending, no matter what. In the end, the guy and girl that argued all the time would find common ground and live happily ever after, the opposite of what was happening here.

Chapter Six
Ryker

Ryker had put in more steps walking around his own damn house today than he had in weeks doing anything else. He paced his living room after Catherine had left this morning, debating what to do. He wanted to know who she was going out with tonight, just to make sure she was safe, or so he told himself.

Then he'd paced his office as he waited for any word on the investigation into the woman claiming to have a kid by him. Catherine had helped ease his concerns over that, but he was still pissed off about it. Never before had anyone tried this, and he wasn't handling it well.

He also felt bad for the kid. Clearly, his mother had issues and would probably run all kinds of scams with the kid in tow, using the kid for her own gain. It was truly awful what some people would do just to pull a con.

Hours after Catherine had left his house, Cade called. Secretly hoping for info on Catherine's date, Ryker answered.

"Hey," Cade said. "What are you doing?"

Pacing the house because your sister is on a date without me. "Not shit. What's up?" He decided that was the safer answer.

"Wanted to see if you wanted to come by for dinner with us?" Cade asked.

"Not tonight," he declined without hesitation. Someone needed to be watching out for Catherine.

"Okay? You good?" Cade asked.

"Yeah. Just dealing with some work shit and I don't feel like socializing tonight," Ryker explained. It wasn't an actual lie.

"It wouldn't have anything to do with my sister being on a date, would it?" Cade drew out the question as he spoke.

"What? No! That's, why, whatever," Ryker sputtered out before giving up on forming a complete sentence.

Cade just laughed. "That's what I thought. Let me know if there's anything I need to know."

Ryker ended the call. There was nothing more to say to his so-called friend. Cade had given him the go ahead to date Catherine but Ryker knew it would be a disaster waiting to happen and Catherine could and would do so much better than him. Someone who didn't have random women accusing him of knocking them up.

Deciding he needed to do something, he opened the email from Kayla with the link to everything he needed to set up for his own date. The best distraction would be another woman, right? Someone to take his mind off his neighbor.

It didn't take as long as he thought it would to fill out the personality survey. He even answered the questions honestly. Just for shits and giggles, he'd love to know if that test had even matched him with anyone, but wasn't going to ask.

He missed Catherine leaving, deep into working on a project he was thinking of taking on. Not that it was a bad thing, but he wondered what she would wear to her date. Would she cover up or show herself off? It was in the dark, but what if she was hoping to meet the guy after?

God, what if she brought the guy back to her place? She wouldn't do that, not on the first date. No, there was no way.

He was slowly, or perhaps not slowly, turning into a creep about this, but he couldn't shake his feelings. Even though he knew he wasn't the right person for her, he couldn't seem to let her all the way go, either. It was a dick move, and he knew it. At least he wasn't leading her on. He just needed to mind his business.

No sooner had he reminded himself that she wasn't his business than did a car door close outside. Despite his better judgement, he was out of his seat and looking out the window.

She wore a dark dress that hit her just at the knees. If she stood on a grate, she'd give a great Marilyn Monroe impression with how flowy it was. The top of the dress covered her well, with almost long sleeves and a modest neckline. He couldn't help but be taken in by her.

While he'd been admiring her dress, Catherine had looked up and caught him watching. He caught her gaze and swore. She turned away from her own door and headed to his.

There was no point in pretending he didn't know she was coming. On a sigh, he headed for the door to let her in and probably get an earful on minding his own business.

"What the hell, Ryker?" she said as she brushed past him and walked inside. "You waited for me to get home?"

"No."

"Just convenient timing for you to look out the window?" she snapped.

"I heard you close your door. It's quiet in here."

"Did you watch me leave, too?" she asked.

Thankfully, the truth was, he missed it. "No."

"Ugh." She threw her hands in the air and then walked over to his bar, setting her purse down. "Do you have wine?"

"Red or white?" Ryker asked, walking into the kitchen and getting out two glasses.

"Whatever," she waved her hand.

"Was it that bad?" Ryker found himself asking before wincing. "Sorry, I wasn't prying on purpose." He wanted to know, yeah, but he was more concerned that it didn't seem to go well.

"This is why I don't date. Men are idiots." She took the glass of white wine he offered her and took a long sip.

"Present company excluded, of course," Ryker teased.

Catherine arched one eyebrow at him. "I think you said included wrong."

Surprised, Ryker choked out a laugh. "Indeed." Still smiling, he walked around the bar and sat next to her. "What happened?"

"He was an asshole. Just a self-centered piece of shit. I swear, at one point, I thought he was going to tell me how long his dick was. I got all his stats, height, weight, and net worth. It was so annoying." She let out an exasperated sigh.

Ryker didn't know what to say, so he sipped his own glass of wine.

"I should have known when he didn't want to chat in the app that he'd be an idiot. I made rules, and I bent it for this first date, and I knew better." She tipped her glass up and drained the rest of the wine.

Ryker didn't know what to say or how to react. He sat there beside her, motionless, not even touching his own wine, and waited for her to make the next move.

"You know, I don't even know why I bothered. It's like I only attract idiots even on a dating site when they can't see me. Why else would my profile match me with someone like him? It's because that's what is meant for me," she sighed. "Going to drink that?" Catherine pointed at his glass.

Ryker shook his head.

She picked up the glass and drained that one, too. "Now I'm sitting here with the guy who refuses to be with me, explaining my shit attempts at having a love life. What the hell is wrong with me?"

Hoping that was rhetorical, he stayed silent. There was nothing wrong with her, but he didn't know how to handle this version of Catherine. It was also becoming increasingly clear that this wasn't the only alcohol she'd had tonight.

"I told Kayla it was shit. I don't know if I want to do another one.

Maybe I will tomorrow, but tonight just sucks." She stood, wobbled a little, but righted herself. "I'm going home."

Ryker jumped up. "Sit down. I think you could use a glass of water."

"I have water at home. Men suck. I want to go back to my books." She whined, but she sat down.

"Did you eat at the restaurant?" he asked her as he filled a glass for her.

She shook her head. "I mean some salad. It's weird eating in the dark. I'd love to see a cost analysis of food waste there. It is so strange. Have you done it yet?"

He handed her the glass. "Drink this. And no, I haven't. My turn is now. I think I'm waiting for someone to be loaded in for me."

"Hmmph. Probably Luke's choice, so you'll know what a shitty date is soon enough."

Ryker chuckled as he pulled out two pieces of bread and set about making her a sandwich. She needed something to help absorb all the alcohol she'd drank, and this was all he could make quickly.

"Is that for me?" she asked, pointing at the sandwich.

"Do you want it to be?" He couldn't resist teasing her.

She stuck her tongue out at him. "It is for me."

He nodded and handed over the sandwich to her. "Eat that and see if you don't feel a little better after."

"I need actual food," she said around bites. "I love a good salad, but as a side, ya know?"

He laughed as he cleaned up the small mess he made. "I think I can relate to that one."

"Good."

A half an hour of chit-chat passed before he was comfortable that she'd be okay at home and maybe tomorrow less hungover before he walked her to her door. She invited him in, but he declined, knowing full well where his thoughts went at that invitation that it was not a good idea.

"Good night, Cat," he said before walking down her steps.

Ryker

"Why do you call me that?" she asked suddenly.

"Because it suits you," he answered without turning around.

It had been a weird fucking day, and he needed to cool off. Grabbing a beer from the fridge, he carried it out into the cool night where he relaxed on his patio, thinking of all the things that couldn't be.

Chapter Seven
Catherine

Catherine avoided Ryker in person since she'd made a fool out of herself after her shitty date. There was no reason she should have unloaded on him and it hadn't been her intention when she saw him looking out of his window when she got home.

Then she'd used him as a sounding board, confident that he would largely just let her vent. Sometimes her friends wanted to offer help instead of just listening, and that's what she wanted right now. Just to vent about how miserable it was.

Ryker had awkwardly met her need to just listen and then had made her feel better. It was so strange and she couldn't let it go. She was also way too embarrassed to see him in person after that show of insanity.

Working on his PR campaign, though, she had spoken to him. To his credit, he hadn't brought up that night or even hinted at it. Everything had been professional, and he'd not pressed her. She expected him to at least crack a joke, but nothing.

She had put together a few plans for him to review and tonight, a full five days after she lost her mind at his place, was the first time she'd see him in person. With any luck at all, Ryker would maintain the same level of professionalism he had so far.

As far as the date went, she had unmatched with the guy right away. Kayla had convinced her to try at least three dates, so now she was waiting on a new match. If this guy didn't chat with her, she was sticking to her rule, no exceptions.

"I'm heading out now," Jack poked into her office. "You meeting with Ryker tonight, still?" He wiggled his eyebrows in innuendo.

"You know, I'm just not going to tell you things anymore, so you can't use it against me," Catherine teased.

"We both know that's not true. I will assume that you are meeting him." He looked her up and down. "Hot outfit, nice choice."

Before she could throw something at him, he continued down the hall, laughter spilling as he went. Catherine rolled her eyes, but couldn't help sitting a little straighter, knowing that she looked good in her outfit.

Shortly after, she got an alert from the app that she had been matched again. Catherine took a deep sigh before opening it up, unsure if she even wanted to. The match had come with a request to chat.

"Finally," she muttered. A real date with a chance to get to know someone.

> Catherine: Hi. Nice to meet you, kinda.

She sent the message off and cringed. How could she know exactly what to say in every scenario in her life except dating? That was so lame.

> ?: Definitely only kinda.

> Catherine: Yeah, sorry. Lame opener. This is my first time here.

?: This is my third attempt at a date. You are the first time I've had a chat, though.

Catherine: In complete honesty, I did have one date, but they refused to chat and I decided never again without chatting first.

?: Smart. I may use that as my own rule if this doesn't work out. Glad I passed your first test.

Catherine: Feel free to use the rule if needed.

?: I have a late work meeting shortly. Can I message you more later?

Catherine: I actually have one, too, so that works out great.

That was awkward, but seemed to end on a decent note. Maybe that was all the ice breaking that needed to be done and they could be conversational after this.

Pushing the thoughts of the date to the side, she gathered her things to head to Ryker's. He was still doing a good job at keeping things under wraps as far as this woman's claims went, but they were meeting in secret.

Right now, they were just neighbors with mutual friends. It wouldn't be weird for Ryker to be seen with her as a PR person because everything looped back just fine. THe moment she started coming to his office, people would assume they were dating, which is unlikely for Ryker to date anyone, much less them be at his office. Or they would assume there's a scandal involving him and go looking for it.

She hadn't had to be secretive with many clients, or at least not to this extent, and she never met them alone and in their home. Ryker is, as always, the exception, not the rule.

Her phone dinged in the elevator, and she pulled it from her bag.

Ryker

Ryker: Anything you don't eat?

Catherine: What kind of question is that?

Ryker: The kind that says I'm hungry and going to feed you, too, so I'm trying to be accommodating.

Catherine: I don't like olives of any kind. Other than that, I'm not that picky.

Ryker: Noted. What's wrong with olives?

Catherine: They're gross and they smell funny.

Ryker: You need to work on that.

Catherine: Don't ask me a question and then get upset because you didn't like the answer.

Ryker: I'm not upset.

She could picture him with his arms folded, tattoos showing, glaring at his phone as she called him out just a little.

Catherine: I'm just leaving the office, so I'll be there soon.

Ryker: No, you won't.

Catherine: I know how long it takes to get home from work.

Ryker: Dammit woman. Start checking traffic.

Catherine: Did you just call me woman?

Ryker: Did you check the traffic?

She rolled her eyes but did as he was telling her. The entire map was red. She wasn't going anywhere in a hurry.

> Catherine: In my defense, it always looks like that.

> Ryker: No, it doesn't.

> Catherine: Whatever. I'll be there later.

She put her phone back in her bag and made her way to the parking deck. Her old apartment wasn't far from the office and she hadn't run into much traffic. Usually, for the short distance, she'd just call a car. Ryker was right, but she'd never tell him she needed to start checking the traffic.

It took her the better part of an hour to get home, but she finally pulled up outside of her house and parked. She hated traffic and definitely should have looked into what it would be like to commute before buying the house. She probably still would have bought it, but at least Ryker wouldn't be reminding her to check the traffic.

"Food's done," Ryker said as he approached her car.

"Thanks." She reached into her car to grab her bags.

"Why do women always come to the office like they're on a trip? This is so much stuff." Ryker complained, but took the bags she had from her to carry.

"One of us has all the things they need, and the other has someone to do it for them," she quipped.

"This all coming to my place?" Ryker asked.

She shrugged. "Might as well." There was no need to carry it inside her house and come back for something. She'd just take it all home at once later.

He sighed, but led the way to his house. Catherine, for her part, just enjoyed the view. Maybe appreciating what was in front of her wasn't so bad when you knew it wasn't going anywhere. It made it easier because there was no chance of being let down. She was already down.

"I made burgers and fries," he said as they walked in.

The smell hit her as she followed him. She didn't know she wanted greasy food today, but judging by the way her mouth was watering, this was about to hit the spot.

"Smells great," she told him.

"I'll carry all this to the living room and bring you your plate."

She waved him off. "I can grab the plates and meet you in there."

Before he could argue, because he definitely would, she turned to the kitchen. Two plates sat nicely on the counter and she grabbed them both, bringing them with her to the living room.

"Thanks," he muttered. "Wine?"

Her face grew hot at the question, but as she searched his eyes for any hint of teasing, she found none. Then again, it would be even less like Ryker to joke around.

"No thanks. Water would be great."

When he returned with the drinks, she was sitting on his floor, her plate on the ottoman, snacking on fries.

"Do you want to go to the table? I just assumed you'd rather be on the sofa, but I didn't mean for you to sit on the floor."

"All good. This is comfortable for me, but I might need a hand up in this skirt. It was hard to get all the way down here."

He looked at her like she'd lost her mind, but just shook his head. "My lawyer has put the request in for the DNA test. He thinks we can do most of this without me ever needing to go to court, if not all of it."

"That's great, actually. I do have a plan made for if you do need to go to the courthouse for anything, since there are always paparazzi out there, though. Hopefully, it won't be necessary."

He nodded. "I still can't come up with where this woman is from. Nothing about her seems familiar and everything that my guy pulled is the same. We've checked everything about her and nothing makes sense."

"She could just be someone that took a lie too far or maybe she needs help, but it doesn't matter because after the DNA test comes back, you'll be good to go. Then we can break the story so she can't later."

"I don't like that part. If the story isn't picked up before it's over, why then announce it?" he asked.

"So she can't blackmail you with it?" Catherine answered him with just a touch of sarcasm.

"I'll think on that part. What else do you have for me?"

She pointed at the stack of papers next to him. "I have statements in there for every type of situation when it comes to this scenario. The plan is to deny and while saying she's a liar, we don't want to actually say that."

Ryker nodded. "I'll look at it when my hands are clean."

Silence fell across the room, and it was as awkward as she expected. Ryker wiped his hands and picked up his phone, typing on it before setting it down again. Not long after, her own phone went off.

> ?: This meeting is boring, just thought I'd
> share that.

Catherine grinned and picked up her phone to write him back.

> Catherine: Mine is awkward for no reason,
> so it could be worse.

"I'll clear the plates." Ryker stood and grabbed both plates before leaving. He was brusque, but it was so hard to tell if something was wrong or if it was just him being him.

While he was gone, her app went off again and she could swear she heard Ryker swore when it did. Maybe he was jealous after all. Well, it didn't matter, it was too late for them.

"Everything okay in there?" she called out.

"Just clearing the dishes. Was there anything else we needed to go over?" he asked. He sounded angry, and a thrill shot through her at the thought of him being jealous.

"You still haven't gone over the papers," she reminded him.

"I'll look these over tonight and let you know if there're any issues. I'm sure it will be fine, but I'll email you tonight."

Catherine nodded and carefully made her way to her feet. Her skirt would be wrinkled beyond repair now, but she stood with no help.

"I'm not sure what just happened, but don't invite me over again if you're just going to rush me off after. I could have emailed you everything to begin with, like we have been doing." She couldn't resist the urge to remind him that her time wasn't his to demand.

"I'm not sure what game you think you're playing, but I'm not interested, Catherine. I suggest you stop it before you can't take it back," he warned.

Catherine stared at him, confusion written on her face. "What the hell are you talking about?"

"Enjoy your next date," he sneered. "Goodbye."

He didn't walk her out or try to stop her as she gathered her things and stormed off. Screw him and whatever he thought was going on. Did he think he could keep telling her how much he didn't want to be with her and she would just keep hanging on forever? She wasn't that pathetic when it came to dating.

Anger rolled off of her in waves as she struggled to get her key in the front door. She shook with rage at being kicked out of his house without so much as a reason. Pissed off, she set all her bags down in the entryway, grabbed a romance book, and headed upstairs.

A bath, a book, and maybe some booze would make this day a little better. Or at least take the sting out of it.

Chapter Eight
Ryker

By the time the next night rolled around, Ryker was seething. He was so pissed he could hardly see straight and was prepared to tear his friends each a new one until he figured out who did it.

He knew the moment he'd sent that message to his own blind date it was Catherine. Her phone had gone off right after and this app had a unique alert sound. Something he hated, so he had turned it off on his end.

He knocked on Evan's door and waited for him to answer. Purposely late, he wanted everyone here before him so he could yell at them all together and hopefully surprise them all.

"Not like you to be late," Jake smiled at him as he opened the door.

Ryker didn't say a word as he brushed past him, headed for the rest of the guys.

"We were wondering if you were coming," Cade said. "Dealing you in, or you want to wait a few hands?"

Cade took in all the men as he chose his words carefully. "I'm not staying. I just wanted to know which one of you did it," he said in measured, careful, even words.

"Do what?" Evan asked.

"I don't need to know, but I'm asking to give you the benefit of the doubt here. I'm not doing anymore blind dates and you can explain to her why." Cade clenched and unclenched his fists as he tried to calm down.

"Dude, we really don't know what you're talking about," Jake said.

Ryker stared at Luke, ignoring Jake and zoning in on his target instead. "Is this funny to you? Or did you do it because you've got some bug up your ass lately and wanted to fuck with me?"

"Do you know her or something?" Luke asked, looking around at everyone else.

"Did you think I wouldn't figure out who you set me up with? What was the fucking plan there? It's only a joke when I know who it is, but if I were you, I wouldn't want to get found out because I'm done with you and your bullshit." Ryker didn't dare round the table and get closer to Luke for fear he really would hit him.

"Hey, let's figure this out," Jake said, trying to play peacemaker.

"Don't bother," Ryker snapped at him before turning back to Luke. "I'm done. Take your secrets and your jokes with you on your way out. I'm not playing your little games anymore and don't come crawling to me when whatever the fuck it is you have yourself wrapped up in catches up to you."

It took everything he had not to grab the table and toss it to the side in a show of anger. Two deep breaths while glaring at Luke and Ryker turned on his heel and walked back out the door.

"Ryker, wait," Evan called after her.

"You really don't want to get involved in shit, Evan. Go back in the house and play poker. I'll catch you when he's not around."

"Who do you think he set you up with?" Evan asked, undeterred.

Ryker laughed. "I don't think. I know. It's Catherine."

"How do you know for sure?" Evan asked.

"I just do," Ryker grunted out.

"Seriously, man? Those were some pretty heavy accusations you just threw out at Luke and while I'm not saying the kid's not an ass, I'm just trying to put it all together since you're both my friends."

Ryker huffed. "If it makes you feel better, I'll tell you. I texted the woman in the app as Catherine and I were eating dinner at my place." He held up a hand, palm out to face Evan. "Nope. Not explaining that one other than to tell you it wasn't romantic. I sent a message and then she got the notification. I heard it. Then she wrote back, and I got the notification."

Evan nodded. "Pretty hard evidence."

"As I said, it was. Aside from that, my date told me she was going to a business dinner, and that's what we were doing. It's pretty fucking coincidental, Evan." He paced as he tried to sort his thoughts out. "To be honest, I'm pretty pissed at Kayla, too, but I know she was just doing what she was told. You can tell her to end this charade now."

Evan nodded and backed away. The threat to Kayla where he was drawing the line. "I'll let her know."

"Thanks. I don't care that this was a fucking joke on me, Evan. I care that it's going to affect her and I hope that no one tells her that happened. I'm not going to date her, even as a joke. It's a shit fucking thing to do and Luke needs to grow up." Ryker squeezed the back of his neck as he spoke.

"You could just date her," Evan said. "You know Cade wouldn't have a problem with it and Catherine already likes you."

"I'm not what she needs, and that's the end of it." Without waiting for a response again, Ryker left Evan staring after him.

He needed to settle this business with the DNA test and then he could go back to fully distancing himself from her. A new house might be in the works for him, one nowhere near Catherine. She was a tempting distraction, but one he wasn't going to pursue.

He wandered a bit before heading home. Of course, Catherine would step out of her own home as he pulled up.

"You're not at poker night?" Catherine asked.

"Don't feel like it," he answered with a shrug. "Good night."

"Wait." she wrapped her robe tightly around her and came down the steps. "Mind telling me what the hell happened yesterday? Are you mad that I have another date? Because as far as I could tell, you and I were on a path to at least being reasonable with each other, and then you practically threw me out."

"I did not throw you out," he defended.

She arched that brow at him again. "Practically did."

"Why? What does it even matter? You're helping me with something simply because you were too nosy to stay the hell out of my mail. Then it will be done, and we won't need to work together anymore."

Catherine took the last few steps until she was close enough to jab one finger into his chest as she spoke. "You aren't going to do this to me. You will not push me out until I get so angry, I walk away. This has nothing to do with working together because that was going fine. This is you caught up on something else and you need to sort it out and I'll try again tomorrow."

"Why are you pressing this? If you don't want to help, then don't. I didn't ask for your help, remember?" She was the most frustrating woman he'd ever dealt with.

"I never accused you, of all people, of asking for help, Ryker. Everyone knows you never would. I just wanted to offer support because you needed something, like it or not, and it was something I do."

"You shouldn't even have known about it. You were being nosy," he shouted.

"You left the papers laying there wide open for me to see," she pushed back. "Besides, I thought we were being friends and helping each other is what friends do."

He growled as she continued to jab one finger into his chest. "I didn't ask you to be my friend. I know your brother, not you. I'm done with this conversation and if you continue to press it, you're going to regret it."

"Oh yeah? Show me what you got then." She dropped her hands to her hips as though daring him to make good on his threat.

Something in him snapped right then. "You're playing with fire, Cat."

"Smoke, maybe."

The smug grin on her face was replaced with confusion as he closed the distance between them with one step. They were now flush against each other.

"You scared, Cat?" he asked, knowing she'd feel his breath when he spoke.

She shivered, and he smiled down at her. No matter what he wanted, he knew she would react to him. He was taking this moment and making it his.

He brought his right hand up to cup her neck, his thumb gently stroking her cheek. Catherine's eyes fluttered, nearly closing before she opened them again.

"Too much?" He was enjoying teasing her.

"N-no," she stuttered.

"Hmm, so maybe this, then?"

Ryker lowered his head, capturing her lips in a kiss. He meant it to be quick, but when she sighed against his lips and opened hers, there was no stopping it.

He deepened the kiss, using his left hand to push the small of her back, moving them even closer. They were no longer touching. They were together, there on the street in front of any neighbors.

Cat moaned, and it took all he had to step back from her. She wobbled as he did, much the same way as when she was drunk the other night. He helped her steady herself and then took another step back as she brought her hand to her swollen lips.

Ryker

"I told you, Cat, you're playing with fire."

Ryker turned and walked into his house, leaving her standing on the street. He didn't want to see any more of her reaction to him. Walking away was the only way to stop himself from taking everything when he shouldn't have taken what he did.

Chapter Nine
Catherine

Catherine didn't look Ryker's way when she left for her date. She certainly hadn't looked out her window, hoping to catch a glimpse of him in his backyard today, either. That wasn't something she would do, never mind that she had.

The man left her confused and tied up in knots. With anyone else, she was confident and sure, with him, less so. Sure, she liked him, but it wasn't like he was the only man she'd ever liked before. It was frustrating.

Now, she was in her car, driving to go on a blind date with another man, and her thoughts still drifting to Ryker. What was it about him that made her completely unable to put him from her mind? Sure, he was hot, in a bad boy type of way, the tattoos on his arms only helping his image, but that wasn't all it was.

The kiss last night had done something in her mind to get everything twisted. Where she was getting better at keeping their relationship slightly more professional, all hope of that today was gone.

At work, even with him, she was confident. She knew what needed to be done, who to speak to, what to say. Catherine could navigate her way through the nastiest of PR crises with ease. Even his, with a mystery baby and woman involved.

Knowing a little bit about the way he'd grown up, Catherine was confident when she saw that letter that there was no way Ryker would carelessly create a child or leave it without a father or any support. He was far from perfect, like everyone, but he held to his own code of conduct that he refused to create a child to grow up the way he had.

"Miss?" A man tapped on her window.

Catherine looked around. She had blanked out the entire trip to the restaurant and was damn lucky she hadn't wrecked. "Sorry." She handed the valet her keys. "I was lost in my thoughts there for a moment."

The man nodded as she climbed out of her car. Maybe she should have hired a driver for tonight, but she hoped that after this date, she would be less distracted by Ryker, maybe even not thinking of him at all.

She stepped into the lobby and smiled at the host. It wasn't the first time she had been here, but it was her first date experience here. Kayla would be upstairs right now and Catherine had already made plans to meet with her after.

"Good evening," the host greeted. He was a short man, making Catherine feel tall next to him, but always smiling and nice to her. In her experience, not all men were okay standing next to a taller woman. "If you'll wait right here, your table is ready, and I believe your date is here as well."

"Thank you," she acknowledged.

He shuffled through the heavy curtain. Catherine decided it was a good sign that her date was early as well. Being prompt was an important quality because it showed you respected the other person's time, solid rule to live by both professionally and personally.

"Ma'am," another man came out of the curtain behind the host. "If you'll follow me."

She stepped through the parted curtain and was quickly

enveloped in darkness. It took her a moment to push down a bit of panic. Turns out she wasn't quite over her fear of the dark. That was a fun thing to find out right now.

"There's a soft glow of light inside, not enough to see your date, or them to see you, but it usually helps settle any nerves about the darkness," the man explained.

A nervous laugh escaped before she could stop it. "Thanks," she muttered.

"If you'll put your hand on my shoulder, I can lead you to your seat." He tapped her hand before placing it on his shoulder.

She nodded before remembering it was dark. He could probably see her if he was facing her because the staff had a form of night vision goggles, but she spoke anyway. "I'm ready."

Catherine steeled her spine before their first step, determined to have a decent night. She wouldn't be kissed tonight, which meant that the lingering feeling of Ryker wouldn't leave anytime soon, but it was a step toward leaving him behind.

"Your table is on our left," the server said. He took her hand and placed it on the corner of the table. "It's a booth. You can just slide in. Your date will be seated in just a moment."

Grateful for a moment to center herself, she slid into the seat and took a few deep breaths. It would be a disservice to her and her date to sit here and think about Ryker, so she did her best to, again, put him from her mind.

"Your table is on the right, sir," came the server's voice again. "It's a booth, so you can slide over once you're seated if you prefer. Your date is across from you."

"Thanks," a deep voice answered, her date.

She felt the table move slightly as he took his seat. He couldn't see her, but she pasted on a welcoming smile anyway, hoping that it showed through in her voice when they spoke.

"I will be right back with your salads. Your water is in front of you in the small glowing light." She heard him leave their table, and they were alone.

"Umm, hi," the man said.

"Hello," Catherine answered. "I had hoped this would be less awkward, but it seems there's no way to avoid it."

He chuckled. "It's completely dark and we are about to eat with a stranger. I don't think there's a way to make it not awkward."

"Fair enough," she agreed. "How was your day?" She decided the best way out of awkwardness was to just push forward.

"It wasn't bad," he answered. "You?"

"Thankfully, it's been peaceful. Not always the case for me, so I like to embrace when it does."

"I can relate. Unfortunately, mine wasn't all peaceful, but it could have been worse."

"That's good," she replied.

The conversation stalled, and she hoped that he would pick it back up, only to sit awkwardly instead. Their salads were delivered with instructions from their server on where to find silverware and how to locate their plate.

Catherine found she wasn't hungry and took charge of the conversation again to avoid hearing him eat. He was definitely chewing with his mouth open and with her hearing heightened by being mostly in the dark, she couldn't stand it.

"What do you like to do when you aren't working?" That seemed like a safe topic.

"I'm not really sure. I mostly work, and occasionally, I go out with a group of guys I know."

She couldn't see it, but she was sure he shrugged. She waited for him to continue, maybe reciprocate the conversation, but he returned to chewing.

Holding back a sigh, she took a bite of her own salad. The rest of the meal was completely quiet, aside from his chewing.

"If you're finished, I can take your plates," their server said.

Catherine jumped a bit at the interruption but gladly handed over her plate.

"When you're ready to leave, you can press the button at the end of the table." He waved his hand over the glowing dot. "And I will come to guide you out."

She nearly told him she was ready to go now, but her date found his voice.

"Thanks. I'll let you know when we're ready," he said dismissively to the server.

More than annoyed, Catherine knew she was done with this date.

"There's a button for each of you," the server said in a too polite tone.

"Thank you," Catherine said.

"Did you want to go out after this?" her date asked. "I know a place down the way and I have VIP seats."

She didn't even try to stop her eye roll. She probably made more than him as it was, and she wasn't interested in partying, much less with him.

"I'm good, but thank you. I think I'll head home after this."

"You don't want to meet?" He sounded offended.

Based on what? She thought. "I have a minimum date rule before I meet anyone, sorry."

"How many?" he grunted.

"As many as I think it takes to get to know the other person."

"You should have said something then. You didn't try to get to know me," he accused. "So, how many dates would it take?"

"Sir. I think I am done here and done with the chatting as well. I wish you the best of luck in finding what you're looking for." She leaned over and pressed the button.

"Ca — I mean you're being a little quick to end things, don't you think? As you said, we don't know each other that well yet."

Stunned into silence at the man almost saying her name, she held her breath as the hairs on the back of her neck stood up. Torn between confronting him and ignoring him when the server showed up.

"Ma'am, if you'll slide to the end of the booth, I can escort you out."

In the end, she stayed silent, getting up and letting their server lead her out. He gave her instructions on letting her eyes adjust before letting her back into the lobby.

She didn't waste any time and made her way straight up the stairs to Kayla. That man had known who she was, and it wasn't supposed to be possible. She hadn't recognized his voice at all, and she was pretty good at remembering people. It helped with her job.

"Catherine?" Kayla asked as Catherine entered her office. "Are you okay?"

"He knew my name," she rushed out. "He said my name, and I don't know who he is. Do I know him?"

Kayla looked shocked and turned to her computer, typing away. "I didn't look up your date since it was done organically. I was curious how it would all work out."

"Not well. It was just annoying, but something is up and I don't know what it is. He shouldn't know who I am, right?" She knew the answer but couldn't help asking again.

"Definitely not." Kayla shook her head. "I don't know him. He signed up about a month before you, but you're his first date. He had other matches but didn't attempt to date them."

"I need to know who it is," Catherine told her friend. There weren't words to explain it, but she just knew something was wrong.

Kayla bit her lip but nodded. "This breaks every rule but come around here."

Catherine stepped behind Kayla's desk and looked at the man on the screen. Dark hair, thin lips, dark eyes. Nothing about him was familiar, but something was. Like maybe she had seen him in passing before but never spoken?

"I don't know him, but he does look familiar. What's his name?"

"Marcus Brockenson," Kayla said.

Catherine took a last look at the photo and went around the desk to take a seat. "I don't know him, or how he would know me. Can you just un-match us?"

"Already done. I don't see anything weird in his profile at first glance. He passed the initial background check. I'm so sorry."

"Don't be." Catherine waved her off. "I'm not sure what happened, but maybe he just recognized my voice. He was annoyed that I didn't want to meet him after our date, but I think it will be fine." She tried to sound more relaxed about it than she was.

"I'm still going to look into it. I would hate if anything else happened or if there's a glitch somewhere."

"Well, for now I'm the only one that this has happened to, so I think you're good. If there's a glitch, let me know and we will get on the PR work ASAP."

"This isn't about work, Catherine," Kayla sighed.

"It will be if there's a glitch," Catherine countered.

"Whatever. Let me send this ticket in to have it looked at by the developers and then we can order real food."

Catherine threw her head back in a laugh. "I love that you know you don't serve real food."

"What else could I serve in the dark? Hardly anyone eats anyway." Kayla shrugged.

"My date did. With his mouth open," she shuddered.

"Gross," Kayla made a face. "Maybe I need to take him off the app entirely."

"Save someone else from sitting in the dark listening to him chew. It was awful."

"Well, what I've learned with the guys is that you always have at least one awful date before you can move on to good ones."

Chapter Ten
Ryker

Ryker snatched his phone off his desk, answering with a gruff, "what?"

"While I disagree with the decision you made based on assumptions, I need to tell you something," Evan explained.

"What the hell is that supposed to mean?" Ryker asked, taking his attention completely away from his computer.

"Your date was never with Catherine. She went out tonight with the guy that she's been talking to."

"Bullshit," Ryker called him out. "I sent her a message and then her phone went off.

"Purely coincidence. Unlikely, but actually a coincidence," Evan continued. "That's neither here nor there, though."

"You're full of shit."

"I promise you, she's eating with Kayla in her office right now. That's not why I called, though. Things didn't go so well."

Ryker stood to pace as he waited for Evan to continue.

"It seems whoever her date was knew her name. You know that's not supposed to happen, but it bothered her enough to rush up to

Kayla and end the date. The guy was also annoyed she didn't want to meet him after."

"Did she know him?" Ryker demanded.

"Kayla broke the rules to show her the guy and his name. She said he was a little familiar but didn't know him or his name. She seems spooked, according to Kayla. I wanted to ask you to keep an eye on her while all of this is going on. I didn't want to tell Cade yet, and since you live next door, I thought you'd be best."

"Yeah," he bit out, his mind whirling with the information. "We looking into this guy?"

"He passed the background check, but I was hoping you could use Hacker Guy to do a deeper one. I don't want anything to happen to her, and Kayla is concerned about it all."

"That's not his name," Ryker said, out of habit. "Send me the information."

"Done," Evan said.

Ryker ended the call and checked his messages for the information. He didn't recognize the man's name either, but that wasn't odd. Typing up another text, he sent the information to Matt, Hacker Guy, who was even saved as HG in his phone now, to get a full check down asap.

HG: How soon do you want this?

Ryker: Like yesterday.

HG: That means putting my research into Luke on hold.

Ryker: Doesn't matter. Drop everything for this.

HG: What did he do?

Ryker: Went on a date with Catherine and scared her.

HG: Someone scared HER? I thought that woman wasn't afraid of anything.

Ryker: Unless you can text and type, I suggest you focus on the research.

HG: Got it. I'll get something to you as soon as I can.

Ryker: What's taking so long with Luke?

HG: I told you, he's in to something but it's buried pretty well. He must have someone else cleaning up his tracks. I only know there's something to look for because chunks of time and messages/emails are missing. Like completely gone.

Ryker: This first and then go back to that.

Ryker dropped his phone on his desk and went to the window to look towards Catherine's. She wasn't home and based on what he got from Evan, he didn't expect her home anytime soon. He was just making sure that no one else was home, either.

Giving twenty minutes later, Ryker took his laptop to a chair by the window so he could at least pretend to get some work done while he waited for her to come home. He'd feel better once he knew she'd arrived safely.

As he looked over the data on the latest company he was looking at acquiring, his mind wandered constantly. Try as he might, he couldn't focus on work. Between the knowledge that Catherine could be in danger again, and the fact that he had blown up at his friends and blew off a date and was wrong about it was bothering him.

He wondered if he should reach out to the woman on the app again in case she still wanted to connect or just give it up. Probably just give it up entirely since there was zero chance he was going to put in an effort to fix something he didn't even know would work.

Passing headlights grabbed his attention. The car slowed by

Catherine's house, ultimately letting out a passenger who crossed the street to another house. Probably just a rideshare service with someone that lived there.

> Ryker: Is she still with Kayla?

> Evan: Yep. Trying to get them to leave now. They're drunk.

> Ryker: Catherine drove, I think. Her car's not here.

> Evan: Well, shit. It's going to be a long night then.

> Ryker: Call her a car.

> Evan: She's refusing to let me. Saying I can drive her home. They are both saying it now. Might just convince them to have a sleepover at this point and save myself the trouble.

> Ryker: Don't leave. I'll be there soon.

He didn't check to see if Evan replied, instead he grabbed what he needed and headed out the front door. If she couldn't drive herself, he'd go get her. Did he need to? No. But Evan wasn't going to make her get in a car, so really he was helping out Evan and Catherine.

The drive was quicker than he expected, and he parked right in the parking garage himself. Valet didn't get to drive his car today, even though he knew they wanted to when they saw it. His black, perfectly restored 1969 Impala was the car that most men only dreamed about.

Ryker parked and stormed into the building, ignoring the host and waiting customers as he made his way to Kayla's upstairs office. He had no idea how Catherine was going to react to him being there, but he was ready for a fight if he needed to give her one. She just needed to accept that she was getting in his car to get home.

"Ryker?" Catherine saw him first and gasped.

"Catherine?" he mocked.

"Why are you here?" Kayla asked. She tripped over something behind her desk as she came around it. "Did Evan tell on us?"

Ryker bit back a chuckle, as that was exactly what happened. "I just heard a certain someone had a bad date and now needed a ride home."

"Evan!" Kayla raised her voice and pointed at her Evan, who was sitting off to the side in the office.

"I want to go home, Kayla," he said.

"Why would you call him?" she sneered, gesturing at Ryker.

"Would you rather I have called Cade?" he countered. "Besides, I didn't call him about y'all being drunk. I told him to keep an eye on Catherine and her place because of the date. He's also having Hacker Guy look into him."

"I should have something by tomorrow," Ryker added, telling Kayla but turning to face Catherine again. "Ready to go?"

"She's not going with you. You're not nice." Kayla poked him in the chest.

"Get your woman," Ryker said to Evan, who looked amused.

"He's nice when he wants to be," Catherine came to his defense.

"You're just saying that because he kissed you the other night," Kayla shot back at her friend.

Ryker was now the one speechless. Kayla giggled and fell into Evan's lap in the chair. Catherine didn't even blush, only serving to prove how much she'd really had to drink.

"Let's go, Catherine," he warned.

"Or what? You gonna kiss me again and then walk away?" she asked.

"Get your things," he growled at her. Turning to Evan and Kayla, he pointed at his friend. "You didn't hear shit."

"Oh, I heard so much and I'm about to hear more when you leave and Kayla tells me the rest."

"I'm not telling you anything," she pouted. "You called him here."

Evan laughed. "Okay, baby."

"Let's go. If you forget anything, you can get it another day." He needed to get out of here before Kayla said anything else or started kissing Evan, both things he didn't want to be around for.

"I didn't ask you for a ride," Catherine muttered.

"Yet you have it," he told her.

She brushed past him and out the door to Kayla's office. Ryker followed closely behind her, ignoring Evan's laughter as it followed him out the door.

Catherine was walking quickly, but Ryker was able to catch her without effort. Just as they stepped out the door, Ryker took her hand in his and pulled her away from the valet.

"I parked in the garage," he told her, leading her away.

She sighed but fell in step. No comments were made until they reached his car.

"You drove this here?" her incredulous voice sputtered out.

"Yeah?" It wasn't like he never drove the car. He just happened to have it out of storage at the moment. He wasn't going to wait for a driver to pick him up to come get her.

She looked it over appreciatively as Ryker opened the passenger door for her. He smiled, knowing she was awed by the car that belonged to him.

"Buckle in," he said before closing the door and walking around to the driver's side.

The engine roared to life when he turned the key. Ryker stayed focused on Catherine, watching as her face lit up as he revved the engine once. He had no idea that Catherine was into cars at all, much less classic ones. She seemed the electric vehicle type over the gas guzzler that was his Impala.

"Tell me about the date," Ryker said as they began the drive home.

She made a disgusted face. "He knew my name! Can you believe that? I didn't know him, though. I don't know where he got my name from."

"How much did you have to drink?" He couldn't help asking.

Catherine shrugged. "Two bottles of wine, I think. I don't know, I wasn't pouring."

"Two bottles?" The shock was prevalent in his voice.

"Maybe." Another shrug. "I don't know."

"You're going to hate yourself tomorrow," he told her.

"Doesn't matter." She shifted in the seat to face him. "Why did you kiss me?"

Ryker choked. He damn near wrecked the car as he tried to recover. "Damn Cat, warn someone before you just jump into things."

"Why? You didn't warn me."

Well, fair enough. "Because I wanted to then."

"So you don't want to now?" She just went for it.

"Can we talk about it tomorrow when you're sober?" And hopefully she wouldn't actually ask anything, or maybe remember this entire night.

"No. I want to know. It wasn't fair for you to do that to me and then just walk away. What do you want from me?"

Ryker sighed as he parked the car in front of his house and turned to face her. "You."

"Me? What about me? I'm tired of this back and forth."

"All of you. Something I can't and won't have," he admitted, turning back to face the windshield.

"Why not?"

"You know why. You deserve someone better than me. Someone that will fit in your perfect little world, not make it more difficult."

She studied him. He felt her gaze burning into him. "You actually think that, don't you?"

"Go home, Catherine."

"I'll go home with you." She grinned at him.

Ryker cursed whatever entity had cursed him with having this woman throw herself at him only for him to not be able to act on it. She was too drunk and in the daylight tomorrow she'd regret everything.

"Not tonight." He shook his head and got out of the car.

Catherine started speaking the second he opened her door. "We will continue this conversation tomorrow."

She'd be lucky to function tomorrow. "Okay," he placated.

He watched as she let herself in her house and listened for the door to lock. Once she was safely at home, Ryker made his way to his. It was going to be a long night, reminding himself that he couldn't act on their urges.

A cold shower was his next step for the night and hopefully some work after now that Catherine was home. He doubted it, but he was going to try to do anything to get his mind off her.

Chapter Eleven
Catherine

Catherine stretched as she waited for her coffee to brew and thought about yesterday's events. All in all, the evening hadn't been terrible, even after her weird date. Hanging out with Kayla and blowing off some steam was exactly what she needed.

Then there was Ryker coming to her rescue and saying she wanted her when her drove her home but sending her home alone. She was drunk, no denying that, but why did he admit it to her then?

Hangovers were never a big deal for her. She knew how to take care of herself before bed no matter how much she had to drink and this morning and a few headache pills and a bottle of water had solved her problem. After coffee, she was going to solve another, her neighbor.

Ryker had likely thought she wouldn't remember anything from last night. She was feeling good but was nowhere near blackout drunk. He was about to have a surprise and some explaining to do, just as soon as she was caffeinated.

Knocking at her front door had her heart racing. Quickly, she dialed the police number on her phone and hovered her finger over the call button. Better safe than sorry, and while the guy from last night was probably harmless, she wasn't taking chances.

Peeking through the peephole on her door, she sighed in relief at Ryker standing there. The man wasn't going to wait for her to have her coffee.

She unlocked the door and pulled it wide, uncaring about the pajamas she had on or her lack of makeup. Ryker looked her up and down with what felt like an appreciative glare before stepping inside.

"Close that and lock it back," he told her.

"Yes, sir," she muttered, doing it and then following him into the kitchen.

"I brought you a breakfast sandwich." He held up a bag.

Her stomach growled. She hoped it was a greasy mess because that was always what she wanted after a night of alcohol.

"Thanks." Catherine took the bag and set it on the counter. "Coffee?"

Ryker nodded, and she poured them both a mug and settled at the bar to open the sandwich. It was a biscuit piled with bacon, processed cheese, and eggs, exactly what she needed. She dug in without a second thought.

"How are you feeling this morning?" Ryker asked as she ate.

"Fine," she answered between bites.

He grunted like he didn't believe her.

Catherine gave him her best smile and motioned to the chair beside her. "Have a seat."

It didn't take him long to take the seat next to her, turning to face her. "We need to talk."

She nearly snorted. They definitely did. "I agree."

"I have information on both the guy from last night and some updates from my lawyers on my case."

Oh, they were going to do work first and pretend last night didn't happen? "Okay. Do you have it so I can look it over?"

"I emailed it to you. Where's your laptop? I can get it for you," he offered.

Catherine pointed to her living room. It was sitting on the coffee table where she had planned to curl up and work yesterday after her date. That didn't go as planned.

"Here." He handed it to her and waited for her to login. "Check the first one I sent. It's about the guy from last night."

She opened the email and looked at the photos first. The top one was Marcus with Luke, clearly partying. It didn't mean much as Luke partied with everyone, so one night wasn't concerning her. It was the next three photos of them partying, clearly different days and different places, that alarmed her.

The fourth photo was Luke and Marcus with their heads bent together, clearly having a conversation. Luke looked angry, and the other man appeared satisfied. She couldn't know for sure, but it seemed like the other man was getting away with something that Luke wasn't happy about.

Sandwich forgotten, she opened the file attached to the email and skipped the rest of the photos. The connection between him and Luke was outlined with a timeframe, noting the missing timeframes from Luke's days, even some whole days that Luke was unaccounted for.

"What is this?" Catherine whispered, mostly to herself.

"between you and me only, I am having Luke researched before this and we keep coming up with blanks in his life. He seemingly disappears, no cameras, no money trail, nothing. I don't know where he goes or what he does. This wasn't related to that until I had your date looked into."

She took a moment to process that information. "So Luke appears to be working with Marcus and we don't know how or why? Or if it even relates to me?"

Ryker nodded.

"Do we ask Luke directly what the hell is going on? It wouldn't be weird considering how the date went, and that Evan called you. Naturally, we would look into this guy."

"No. Keep reading." He motioned to the screen.

She focused on the laptop again and continued reading. References to what the man did for work and in his downtime. It wasn't pretty, but neither was it alarming. He was basically a wastrel.

The last page made her blood run cold. Connections between their families. Her father and his father meeting repeatedly and then the son joining them. Meeting details appeared not to be available, but both father and son had visited her father recently in jail.

"Why is he even allowed guests?" she wondered aloud. "This is the man that my father wanted me to marry for his business deals. Why is he still allowed to try to control this from there? It doesn't make any sense." Her voice rose with each word until she was yelling.

Ryker didn't ask her to calm down or jump in to her thoughts. He let her have her moment of freak out and didn't question when she took a few deep breaths and settled down again.

"I need to call a lawyer and get his visitation stopped." She reached for her phone.

Ryker laid his hand on hers, stopping the movement. "This is all speculation right now. I don't like it, but you're only going to show your hand if you do something now. Let's see what else we can turnover. I have him looking into what he's up to now."

She didn't like it, but she nodded. "I know you're right, but I hate it. The worst part is that if this dude hadn't been a straight jerk, I might have actually met him sometimes. All the while, he was conspiring with my father. What even is the point in dating anymore? It always somehow comes back to my father." Tears threatened, but she held them back. "Why is he still impacting my life?"

Now, Ryker put an arm around her shoulder and squeezed her into his. "I don't know. We will figure it out and I won't let anything happen to you."

She believed he would try to keep anything bad from happening. No one could really promise no bad would happen, but he was determined, and she appreciated it. A few tears slipped as she pulled away from him, wiping her cheeks.

"You said there was news in your case, too?" Anything other than her own messy life would be great.

He cleared his throat and nodded. "The other email."

Catherine had to blink the tears away a few times before she could see straight and click on the email. Again, she went to the pictures first and looked at both the woman and the baby. There were candid shots, and some that had been posed for.

The woman was pretty, exhausted, but you could tell if she got some rest, she was model material. The child was cute, but bared no resemblance to the man next to her as far as she could tell.

The documents attached were a birth certificate, with no father listed, bank statements that were surprisingly healthy, and the DNA test results. It proved what they had known all along: Ryker was not the father.

"This is good, right?" She smiled at him.

"I think so." He took a deep breath. "I want to know why this happened and then I want to make sure that kid is taken care of."

She squinted her eyes as she studied Ryker. "Why? It looks like she has plenty of money." She pulled the bank statements to the front.

Ryker nodded. "Indeed. But that's not what I'm worried about. I think there may be drugs involved here."

"Why?"

"Where else would she get that kind of money?"

He had a point, again. "You're going to keep watching and see before you make that decision, right?"

Ryker didn't get to answer as a furious pounding on her door interrupted their conversation.

"Catherine! Get out here! You owe me, and I'm not just going to let this go!" The man on the other side of the door shouted.

"Stay here," Ryker told her, shifting to stand.

"Like hell," Catherine replied.

He rolled his eyes and sighed. "At least stay behind me?"

Catherine nodded. She'd try. She didn't need to say that out loud and provoke him, though.

Chapter Twelve
Ryker

He wished that for once in her life the woman behind him would have listened to him. He didn't want her to be in the middle of whatever happened when he got to that door and, while he preferred to swing it wide open and confront the man, he would not do that with Catherine so close.

"Tell him to go away," Ryker whispered.

She swallowed and then shouted at the man. "Leave me alone!"

"We had a deal. You aren't getting out of it by being a stuck-up bitch."

"I don't have any deal with you," Catherine yelled again.

Ryker stayed poised to cover her mouth if she took things too far, but getting some information from the man would not hurt just yet.

"You are the deal. Now open up and let's get this show on the road."

Catherine eyed Ryker, who shook his head. "Tell him you'll call the cops if he doesn't leave." Ryker was facing her now, holding her against him.

"I'm going to call the police if you don't leave." Her voice shook a little as he assumed the reality of what was happening started settling in.

"Go ahead. It's nothing a few threats and a bit of money won't solve. I'll be back soon and you better be prepared to accept the reality that is coming your way."

Ryker leaned his head against hers, willing her to stay quiet. After he felt like enough time had passed, he stood and looked through the peephole, confirming he couldn't see anyone.

"Go pack everything you need. We still have a lot to sort out, but you're staying with me until then." Ryker grunted it out and stepped away from her.

Catherine opened and closed her mouth a few times before nodding and walking away. He imagined it was her war of indecision as his order before accepting that it was the best idea. And it was. She couldn't stay here alone.

> Ryker: The guy came to her house. We need to know what the deal is asap and how the hell this guy was able to get a date with her specifically.

> HG: On it.

> Ryker: Taking her to my place. We'll both be there if you need us.

> HG: I would have known when I needed to.

Ryker rolled his eyes and headed to the kitchen. He wasn't sure if she had a maid service coming in, so he cleaned up from their coffee and her breakfast. No need to leave it all sitting out, and he didn't think she'd come back for the sandwich after what just happened. If she wanted another one, he'd get it for her.

She took her time getting ready to go. Fifteen minutes after he'd told her to pack a bag, Ryker was still waiting. One hip leaned on the counter as he debated going upstairs to check on her. He didn't think the man had come back or that he wouldn't have heard it if he did.

"I'm ready," Catherine called from the top of the stairs. "I wasn't sure what to bring, so I brought comfy clothes and then I can come over here to get ready for work in the morning if I need to."

That defeated the entire purpose of what they were doing, but he didn't argue with her. If he could manage it, he'd keep her home tomorrow and by his side until all of this was settled, anyway. If she didn't have anything to wear to work, well, that just only made it easier for him.

"I've got your computer. I don't want to do a lot of back-and-forth today, so are you sure you have everything you need for now?" He hoped that no one saw them bringing her things to his place.

"Actually, I was thinking that maybe we should take my luggage and maybe me through the back gate instead of out front." Catherine hit the last step with her luggage.

"Not a bad idea, but I can't watch you from there, and I don't want to leave you alone." The thought of her alone for a minute and that man showing back up was too much.

"I'll stay locked inside and you go around and meet me at the gate. You can call me when you're ready."

"No." Ryker stayed firm. "Let's just go."

She didn't continue to fight him on it, and he was grateful. He took her suitcase in one hand and slid the laptop into her arms. When they reached the front door, he took her hand and hurried to his own front door.

"You need a better security system. One with cameras," Ryker commented once they were in his house.

"I don't want cameras in my house."

He could understand that. It wasn't what he meant, though. "I mean outside, front and back. I want video of him if he shows up again."

"Oh," Catherine said quietly.

"Going silent on me?" Ryker pressed, trying to get Catherine back to her usual self.

"Thinking of who I can call to have a system installed." She didn't have a comeback for him, and he hated that. Their banter was something he enjoyed as much as it annoyed him.

"I'll arrange it. I have vetted companies I use already."

"Thanks. I'll go put this in the same room I used before?"

Ryker nodded and let her go. He wanted to go with her, wanted to follow behind her, carrying her bag and assuring her that this wasn't the end of the world and that he'd protect her.

He knew Catherine, though. Very few times had he ever seen her like this: stoic, nothing to say, and he knew that meant she needed some alone time. He'd arrange the security system and then check on her.

It took half an hour to get someone to agree to come out today to set the system up. He threw enough money at the problem to have it installed before dark on a Sunday. The cameras would work day and night and record everything.

"Catherine?" Ryker gently rapped his knuckles on her door. "I have someone coming to set up the system today."

She sat on the bed, facing away from him. "Thanks."

Taking a chance, he stepped into the room and went to her. "It's okay," he soothed. "We will get this figured out."

"I know," she said, her voice flat. "It's what to do in the meantime that bothers me."

"What do you mean?" he asked.

"That was my house. It was supposed to be me moving on from my father and all the things that happened in that apartment, and now it's happening again." Tears flowed in earnest when he stood in front of her.

"Baby," Ryker pulled her to a stand and wrapped his arms around her. "It's all going to be okay, and you won't have to go through this alone. I won't let anything happen to you and we will get this guy."

She nodded into his shirt and tried to pull away. "I'm making your shirt wet."

"I don't care. I have more shirts, use as many as you need." He'd hand her each one to use as a tissue if she wanted it.

He was rewarded with a small laugh from her. They stood there for a few more seconds and when she tried to push away this time, he didn't resist.

"Thank you," she said.

He watched, mesmerized by her as she closed her eyes and took three deep breaths, shook her head, and opened her eyes back up as a different person. Gone was scared and unsure Catherine, back in her place was the everyday Catherine that was confident and sure of herself.

"I needed that," she told him. "Now let's get to work."

She flew from the room. There was no other way of saying it. It was like her feet never touched the floor. Laptop in one hand, he followed her down to his living room, where she was already making herself at home, again.

"There are implications if you decide to help this woman now that you can prove the baby isn't yours. I want to get ahead of things just in case that comes out."

Ryker took a seat and listened, without actually understanding. He was caught up in the way that she was able to transform herself and how he, too, was completely confident in her abilities here. He agreed or grunted when it seemed like a response from him was needed.

"Ryker!" Catherine swatted him. "You aren't listening."

"Yes, I am," he countered, knowing full well he hadn't heard shit.

"I just asked if my hair was turning green and you agreed with me." She rolled her eyes. "I don't need your input, anyway. I'll just make a plan and send it to your lawyers if the time comes."

That's what she would have done anyway, but he didn't tell her that. "Sure," he agreed. "What do you want for lunch?"

"Something greasy still? I didn't get to finish my breakfast sandwich."

"Fries?" he offered, knowing she loved them.

She nodded. "Mm-hmm. With cheese."

Ryker laughed. "Why aren't you hungover?"

Catherine stopped typing and over at him, connecting their gaze. "I wasn't as drunk as you assumed I was."

Ryker felt a knot develop in his stomach, but didn't let her see it. "Well, good for you. I believe that Kayla was."

"Probably," she said noncommittally.

He took his opportunity to escape her closeness as he remembered what he'd told her last night. Either she didn't remember it or was doing a damn good job and pretending she hadn't heard him. Had he seriously confessed his feelings for her even a little bit?

Ordering them both some lunch, Ryker kept his distance from her until the food arrived. Beyond a few passing words, even lunch was quiet. The security system took up some of his time while that was installed and before he knew it, he was alone for the night with Catherine looking very much like that the next words out of her mouth were going to piss him off.

Chapter Thirteen
Catherine

Catherine waited for Ryker to return from her house for the last thirty minutes. He'd been avoiding her since she told him she wasn't that drunk last night. He had gone from super supportive to missing in the flip of a switch.

Well, she wasn't having it anymore. Once the security system was in place, he had no other reason to avoid her and they were going to have the conversation she'd wanted to have with him since before he showed up that morning.

Tomorrow she'd be going home no matter Ryker's opinion. She would not let this man run her from her home and, with a security system in place, she'd be safer. She doubted Ryker had even realized that he'd given her a reason not to stay by installing the system.

She was oddly excited to see how their night would go.

Ryker pushed open the front door and stepped in, locking it before noticing her. He took her in from head to toe and back up again. She thought there was desire in his eyes, if only for a moment.

On a sigh, Ryker spoke. "What now?"

"Honestly, it's a wonder I don't develop some kind of complex with how hot and cold you are to me." She spoke her thoughts out loud. "We need to talk, Ryker, and then we can decide where things will go from there."

"I have things to do." He attempted to go around her.

Catherine sidestepped to be in front of him again. "No, you don't. You didn't even need to be over there for the system to get set up. Don't give me that. You and I are going to have a real conversation tonight."

"What do you want?" he asked.

"I want to know more about what you said to me last night when you thought I wouldn't remember. I want to know why you think you are doing either of us a favor by ignoring what's clearly there between us in some sort of sacrificial penance?"

His nostrils flared as he struggled to maintain control of his emotions. She didn't want him in control, she wanted him to let go, tell her what he actually wanted.

"I want to know what the hell is so wrong with me or you we have to pretend that there's no way we could work? Because, Ryker, you know we'd be good together."

"You don't need to get caught up in my shit," he protested.

"No. You don't get to make that decision for me and without my input. If you don't want me, then fine. That's fair, and I'll leave you alone without another question. But, if you were worried about me and your business, don't forget that I'm already involved and tonight will mark the second night I've slept over in your house, whether or not we sleep together."

Ryker took a step back from her and Catherine followed him, keeping him close. That was all it took to push him over the edge.

His hands came up to her neck and hair as his mouth crushed hers. This was nothing like it was the other night. It was more, powerful, with no end in sight. Catherine reveled in it, giving what she got and taking what she wanted from him.

He slid his hands down her back, gripping her ass and lifting her against him. She wrapped her legs around his low back, letting him lift her completely off the ground.

He broke the kiss and rested his forehead on hers. "Be sure this is what you want before we go any further," he warned.

Catherine growled against him. "If you stop, I will murder you in your sleep."

His laughter rumbled through her as his chest shook. Then they were moving. Ryker carried her upstairs to his bedroom, dropping her not so delicately on the bed.

Ryker wouldn't be gentle, and she smiled at it. She didn't want gentle, not from him. There was a time and a place for it, but not between them as they finally reached the end of everything they'd danced around for years.

He unbuttoned his shirt, watching her laying on his bed. She raised up on her elbows to see him better as he did. Knowing what he looked like when swimming was different than having it bared just for her alone.

"Undress," he commanded.

With anyone else, she would have bristled at the tone. With Ryker, she found it sent a pulse of heat through her and she was obeying him without even thinking about it.

He stopped undressing and watched her. His hands were at his belt, but he made no moves to undo it. Catherine watched, waiting for him to move as she threw her own shirt off her head and to the floor.

"Bra, now." Another command. At this rate, she was going to get off just with him, telling her what to do.

She tossed her bra to the side and laid back down. Ryker came to her and leaned over the side of the bed, spreading her legs wide, grinding his erection against her.

Whimpers filled the room as Catherine struggled to breathe at the promise of what was to come. He felt so good and hadn't done a damn thing yet.

Both hands grasped her breasts, squeezing and kneading them as his eyes stayed on hers. He rolled one nipple and Catherine tossed her head back, breaking the eye contact in pure pleasure.

"You like that?" he asked.

Catherine didn't answer, didn't think she could answer. Then he stopped.

"I like it when you talk to me. Tell me what you want, Cat."

"Please?" she begged.

"What do you want?" he demanded.

"Your mouth on me," she all but shouted. She needed him on her now.

"Close enough," he said before bending down and doing what she asked.

He lavished each breast one at a time. His mouth devouring her, biting and pulling on her nipple before giving her relief. It was a pleasure pain she didn't even know she liked. His hand stayed busy working the other breast each time.

"Can you get off from just this?" he asked.

"I don't know," she managed. Right now, she felt like she could combust. Never had it been like this before from just breast play. She wouldn't be surprised if she came from just this.

"Another time," he ground out.

His hands slid to her waist, pulling her pants and panties off in one yank. He pulled her to the edge before going down on his knees, his tongue darting out and licking her slick folds.

Catherine gripped the bed covers when his hands went under her thighs and around, pulling her to him and holding her still. His mouth assaulted her senses as he licked and teased her.

She tried shifting, knowing where she needed him, but it seemed Ryker was determined to play with her. Just when she was prepared to tell him what she needed, his mouth closed over her clit and he grazed his teeth across.

Nothing else was needed. She was seeing stars. She cried out, lost to the passion and not caring that she was being loud. Ryker stayed between her legs, letting her ride him through the wave of pleasure until she floated back down.

Her eyes fluttered open just in time to see him back away and drop his own pants to the ground. A condom appeared from somewhere and she marveled at him pulling it on.

He was going to fill her like she couldn't ever have imagined, his shaft long, yes, but swollen around it looked like some toy she'd never dreamed of using. She'd be ruined after this, nothing but him would do it and she knew it.

Catherine stayed where she was as Ryker moved to stand between her legs. He didn't ask again if she was sure, he just went for it. One thrust had her gasping as she stretched around him.

He stayed still, giving her a moment to adjust to his size. When she did and he didn't move, she nodded at him.

Given the go ahead, Ryker slowly slid almost completely from her before thrusting in again with the same quickness as before, but with more force. She wanted to reach for him but couldn't let go of the blankets as another wave of pleasure was building in her again.

Ryker continued his pattern before he slid completely from her. His hands slid under her and slipped her over, spreading her legs wide and guiding her head to the mattress.

"Fuck," he shouted as he thrusted back into her again.

He quickened the pace, roughly taking her over and over again as Catherine whimpered and moaned into the blankets. It didn't take long before she felt herself ready to come again. Not wanting to hold back, she let it happen, quickly falling back over the ledge as she shouted his name.

Ryker followed right behind her, his own shout more of a roar as he held himself still, deep inside of her. They stayed there for a moment, panting, recovering from the sheer power of what happened before Ryker pulled from her.

She collapsed onto the bed as he rose from it, returning a moment later. He moved the covers back and then lifted her up, placing her on the sheet before sliding in next to her and pulling her to him. Covers fell over them both as she drifted somewhere between sleep and awake.

Ryker kissed the top of her head.

Ryker

"Who knew I liked it rough?" Catherine joked.

"I did," Ryker said proudly.

They both laughed lightly at his confidence.

"That you did," she yawned.

"Sleep, Cat. I've got you."

She did. The deepest sleep she'd slept in a long time. Curled into him with his arms around her, she'd never felt more safe and relaxed.

Chapter Fourteen
Ryker

Ryker held Catherine close in his arms the next morning. He should let her go, demand that she leave and keep her from everything that was him, but he couldn't bring himself to do it just yet.

She was too perfect to be his, but she'd made it clear last night that she wanted this, anyway. He was going to do his best to keep her safe while keeping her sated. Maybe if they kept up like they had last night, she'd be too busy to get in to anymore trouble.

"That tickles," she groaned, swatting at his hand, that had been gently rubbing small circles on her back.

He rumbled out a laugh. "Are you not a morning person? I always assumed you were."

She turned over onto her back from the spot that she was curled in next to him, tucking the sheets around her breasts. "I am normally a sleep person and I didn't get much of that last night."

"You weren't complaining then," he teased.

"I'm not complaining now. I was just explaining why I'm not a morning person today." She threw one arm up and over her eyes, blocking out the sun that was creeping into the room.

"Will coffee help?" He already knew the answer.

"Yes, please." She shifted and removed her arm, staring at the ceiling.

Ryker leaned over and pressed a bruising kiss to her lips. "Go shower and I will make you some coffee."

"My hero," she joked.

Ryker puffed out his chest as he stood, grabbing sweats to slip on from the drawer. "Damn right."

He caught a glimpse of her in the mirror on his dresser as she licked her lips while looking at him. Reminding himself that he was going to make coffee, he glanced away before he joined her back in the bed.

Without another glance her way, Ryker left the bedroom and chose not to think on the feelings that were rising up inside of him right now. He didn't want to consider why it felt so right to have her in his arms when he woke up this morning and why he had never felt that with another woman.

Those were thoughts for another time, or never. Ryker made them both a cup of coffee and waited for Catherine to come downstairs to join him. She didn't take long and was fresh from the shower when she came down.

He'd expected her to grab one of his shirts rather than slip into the other room where her things were and get her clean clothes. Disappointment was another thing he was filing away for later thoughts.

"Good morning," Catherine beamed at him.

"Nope," he joked. "Dial it back down some more. Not grumpy like earlier, but this is too much." He held the mug of coffee up out of her reach.

"Come on," she whined, playing along. "Trade you for a kiss?"

"Hmm, I could be swayed." Ryker leaned down and kissed her, setting the mug on the counter.

He felt her hands slide around him, grabbing the cup. "Thank you," she said, pulling away.

They drank their coffee in peaceful silence. He didn't know what to say or what they were supposed to do now, sleepovers with women weren't something he did. And on the rare occasion they happened, he was the guest and just headed out.

"Any updates from Hacker Guy?" Catherine asked.

"I wish you hadn't named him that."

"You know he likes it. Besides, where's the lie?" She grinned as she took another sip.

Ryker slid only a seat at the bar. "No updates yet. That was the update that I got."

"Cade called this morning." She bit her lip. "I didn't answer."

The odds of Cade actually having an issue with what was happening between them was slim. He'd all but told Cade to go for it more than once, but he wasn't an overly involved brother. Knowing that they had gone for it might change his mind.

Ryker pulled out his phone to see if he had missed a call.

> Cade: What the hell is going on with Catherine?
>
> Cade: Why didn't you tell me what was going on?
>
> Cade: Ryker, is she at your place?
>
> Cade: You both better get dressed, I'm on my way over.

He held the phone out for Catherine to read the messages.

She took a deep breath and slowly let it out. "You better go shower, it might be a long day."

"I don't think that he will care about this." Ryker gestured between them.

"Not worried about that. I'm more worried that we didn't tell him about the date or the stuff from yesterday. He's going to lose it."

Ryker stole another kiss before taking his coffee up with him. He'd shower and be back down before Cade got there.

It didn't take him long, as he'd thought and he was taking the last sip of his mug when he rounded the corner into the living room. He was struck by how perfect she looked sitting there on his oversized sofa, hair pushed behind her ears, feet tucked under her.

He leaned against the wall and just took her in until she caught him watching. She blushed and ducked her head.

"Stop," she laughed.

"Why? I can openly appreciate you now," he admitted.

"Mm, appreciating? Is that what you were doing?"

"Indeed." Ryker was almost to her when his doorbell rang. "Stay here just in case. It's probably Cade though."

Catherine didn't listen. He wasn't surprised, but he kept himself between her and the door even after he confirmed it was Cade.

"Come on in," Ryker said sarcastically as Cade rushed past him into the house.

"Sorry about him," April said as she followed him in.

April was pregnant and each time Ryker saw her, she was bigger and bigger. He wondered how much longer she could continue to expand.

"Cade!" April shouted. "You left the pregnant lady way back here."

Cade had the good grace to look sheepish as he left off from talking to his sister and came to help his wife.

Ryler skirted the couple and went to Catherine, making his intentions known when it came to Catherine. Cade would understand it.

"So that's how it is?" Cade asked without missing a beat when he saw them.

Ryker gave a sharp nod.

The moment stayed tense until April and Catherine broke out in laughter.

"It's about time," April teased and wrapped Catherine in a hug. Noticing her husband hadn't moved, she stepped back and elbowed him in the ribs.

"Fine. But you didn't see these two try to avoid getting here for as long as I have. I get to pretend to be angry about it for at last a minute."

Catherine leaned on Ryker's chest, her back touching his entire front. "You don't care."

"I care some." Cade folded his arms and did his best to look menacing. "Actually that's not why I'm here. Tell me what the hell else is going on!"

"Language!" April snapped.

"It doesn't matter yet," Cade argued back.

"It does. It's called practice and you need it." April looked at Catherine before speaking again. "He does own a sofa right?"

"Come on." Catherine looped her arm through April's and led her through to the living room while the men trailed behind.

"Are you serious?" April stood in front of his sofa. "If I get in this, it will take a crane to get me back out of."

Catherine was giggling beside her.

"I will get the best crane money can buy to lift you everywhere you go," Cade said with half sincerity.

April threw him a cutting glare. She took a seat and slid herself back, sighing as she did. "Screw the crane. I want this sofa."

They all laughed at that and took a seat. Catherine quickly ran through everything that had happened in the last few days. It wasn't a lot really, even though it felt like it. She left out the information about Luke. They hadn't discussed that and he wouldn't have been mad if she told him but was happy she didn't.

Cade listened intently, before turning to Ryker. "What else?"

"She actually did a pretty good job of giving you the whole story. There's not a lot to add, except that I am still working to find out how this guy was able to get a date with Catherine. It shouldn't have been able to happen."

"No, it shouldn't have."

"Kayla has given full access to anything we need in order to sort this out."

"Have you checked her phone?" April asked.

"Huh?" Ryker turned to her.

"I'm just saying it's possible that it wasn't an attack on the restaurant security, but more of a personal attack on Catherine. He could have seen what she put in her assessment and then made sure he matched her." April said casually like it was something simple they should have thought of.

Cade and Ryker shared a look.

"What? I've been watching true crime stuff from weeks. I'm bored but well-educated." April shrugged.

"I'm on it." He quickly fired off a text to have Catherine's phone looked in to.

"Well, I feel silly for not thinking of that," Catherine said.

"It's okay. Maybe it won't matter," April tried to reassure her.

Catherine stared at her phone like it held all the answers but she was scared to get them.

"Not going to risk it," Cade said, snatching the phone. "Do something with it." He handed the phone to Ryker.

"Have him check my computer, too," Catherine said.

"Hand it here." Ryker took it from her and carried both devices to his office.

When he returned to the living room, Ryker sat close to Catherine, dropping his arm around her. It felt natural which was alarming since he'd never done that before.

"I can go meet with Father," Cade offered.

"Don't waste your time, he won't tell you anything." Catherine snuggled closer to Ryker. "It'll just leave you angry and no closer to the answers that you were before."

"I advised her to wait to call the police or a lawyer until we can get some more information. I don't want to tip anyone off before we know the whole story, or as much as we can."

"Have you considered taking some time off? Maybe heading upstate for a while and seeing if we can draw this guy out but keep her safe?"

He hadn't considered that at all. "It's an option."

"I don't think we need to escalate him right now." Catherine sounded nervous.

"Think about it. I know that Ryker has some properties that aren't publicly known." Cade stared at Ryker.

"We will do what we need to," Ryker agreed. "And keep you as up to date as possible." He wasn't going to pretend that there wouldn't be other things he'd keep from Cade.

"We have lives, Cade," Catherine said in a tone that sisters reserved for brothers.

"I'm trying to make sure you protect your lives," Cade sneered back at her.

"Not trying to interrupt here, but it's not really your call. I will make sure that she's taken care of." He caught Catherine's glare front the corner of his eye. "And she will make sure I'm take care of."

"That's better," Catherine agreed.

"I have a question," Cade started. "Are you two a couple now?"

April gasped and smacked his arm. "That was rude, you guys don't have to answer him."

Not that he needed her permission not to answer, Ryker found he wanted to. A calming acceptance had settled over him. "We are."

With one finger, he found Catherine's chin, gently tilting her head back for a quick kiss. She smiled back at him. There was still more to be worked out between them, but he was looking forward to it.

"Nope. Not in front of me. Jesus, that's my sister." Cade stood and helped April out of the sofa.

"You're so weird," she complained with a laugh.

"I'm protecting my peace. Time to go before I see something I might need to bleach my eyeballs for." He lifted her up and carried her to the door all while April laughed.

Ryker and Catherine followed them, both laughing along as they did.

Cade set April down and turned to face Ryker. "Take care of my sister," he warned.

Ryker

"With my life," Ryker agreed.

Chapter Fifteen
Catherine

"Ryker?" Catherine called from the kitchen. She was cooking pasta the next evening while he got work done down the hall.

He appeared by her side after a minute. "Smells good in here," he said against her neck.

"Did you order something?" she asked.

"No. Why?" He stiffened and stood straight, looking out the window next to her.

"Someone dropped something off. Looked like a package."

"You saw them?" He spun her to face him.

"It was just a second ago, and yes. But I didn't want to yell for you and spook them and I don't have a phone to text you with." Catherine shrugged and went back to the pasta. Anything to distract her from the mysterious package.

Outside she might be handling it well, but inside, she was freaking out. She didn't want to be freaking out. She wanted to move on with her life and regretted even trying a date.

"For the love of God, woman, stay here this time." Ryker didn't wait to see if she listened.

She had no intention of following this time. Whatever it was, she didn't want it and she didn't need to go out there to know it was for her. Ryker wouldn't be getting anything delivered.

He returned quickly with a brown box about the size of a book and an envelope. "They took a risk leaving it there without ringing the doorbell. Close the blinds."

Catherine did as he said and made sure that the blinds and curtains were closed. "Done. Should we call the police now?"

"I don't want to because it changes how I can operate but I will leave this up to you. If you feel more comfortable getting the police involved, I won't argue."

She thought it over. It meant that nothing that they had done for investigating could be told to them and nothing else could be done. It was all illegal to hack things the way they had.

"You're right," she agreed. "What do we do with this then?"

Ryker opened the envelope and took out a note.

Catherine took a step back. "What if it's poisoned or something?"

"He wants you, killing you wouldn't get him to the end goal," he said as if it were the most obvious thing.

Dearest Catherine,

I know you are unhappy with the way that I had to trick you into a date but I promise you will get over it. You need to stop staying with him and return to your own home so that we can be together. I don't like my wife to be sullied by such a character and you are making me want to do bad things again. I don't want to want to do bad things. Help everyone out and go back to where you are supposed to be.

Your future husband,

M.B.

"What the actual fuck?" Ryker raged.

"I think he's sick in the head."

"Ya fucking think?" He pulled out his pocketknife and opened the box.

Inside the box was a little teddy bear holding a stuffed candy heart that read *Forever Mine*. He looked through the tissue paper in the box and then put it all back inside. Turning to her, he held one finger up to his lips, letting her know to be quiet.

Catherine nodded.

He carried the package out to his backyard and set it on the porch before returning inside.

"That had a small camera on it. He didn't even bother to hide it well."

She wrapped her arms around herself, dinner completely forgotten as she shivered.

"I won't let him get to you. Let me see if we have any updates on your phone." He pulled out his own phone. "I'll order you a new one, regardless."

"Why is this happening?" she whispered.

Ryker curled one arm around her shoulders and led her to the living room and pulled her into his lap on the sofa. "You didn't do anything to make this happen. This guy is just crazy."

She knew that, but it didn't actually make things better. If anything it made her worry about why so many people in her life were like that, her mother, her father, now this guy. It was too much.

A shiver wracked her body and Ryker held her tighter. "You don't have to do anything. I will take care of this guy and everything with that." He kissed the top of her head.

Catherine nodded and rested her head on his shoulder. She hated appearing weak and hated this Marcus guy for making her feel this way. It was great that Ryker was being supportive, but she needed to get herself together.

"Why don't you go take a bath?" he offered. "I don't have bubbles or anything, but it might still be relaxing. I think there are some candles around here somewhere."

It was a good idea. A nice hot soak might help her out of this. "Yeah."

"Yeah?" He didn't waste a second and lifted her up into his arms.

He carried her to his room, setting her on the bed before starting the bath water. He fussed with some things before returning to her.

"You can't take a bath in your clothes," he pointed out.

She stood and Ryker was there to help her undress. He didn't make any moves to do anything else, just tenderly helped her remove her clothes and then led the way to the bathroom.

Bubbles floated in the tub and she let a giggle out at the sight.

"I used some of your soap. Figured it was better than nothing."

"It's perfect," she told him. And it was. She was already feeling more herself.

He kissed her temple and held her hand as she stepped in the tub. "Relax. I'll see you in a bit."

She smiled at him as she sank lower into the water, letting the heat soothe her worries out for now. Ryker closed the door to the bathroom as he left her there.

Her thoughts drifted to the last few days and all that had happened. Ryker was unexpectedly more in tune with her than she thought. She knew they'd be great in bed, but this was more than that.

He was comforting, sweet, and exactly what she needed. They just seemed to work so well together. She couldn't help but wonder if he would remain the same once the threat was gone. Not that she wanted to jinx it but she couldn't shake the thought.

Was this all the time Ryker or the white knight Ryker? It mattered more than anything else right now, and she didn't have an answer. She wished she did, but it was something only time would tell.

He didn't date, ever. He saw women occasionally, but never anything more than once or twice. She only knew that from tabloids and hearing her brother gossip about him. Not that any of their group would admit it, but it was gossiping when they talked about each other.

Cade wouldn't know either. She wondered if anyone had even met the women that Ryker saw, no matter how casual. Luke might have, but he was obviously not one to ask at this moment since he may or may not be involved in this dating disaster.

She slid down the back of the tub and dunked her head, willing the dark thoughts to wash away. Coming up with a deep breath, she pushed her hair out of her face and decided she felt better from soaking.

The water was cooling, and the bubbles had long disappeared by the time she was ready to leave the tub. She made quick work of draining it and getting dressed again.

Ryker was in the living room when she made it downstairs, boxes of takeout spread out waiting.

"What did you order?" she asked as she walked in.

"Chinese. I didn't know what you liked, so I got a little of everything," he told her.

She smiled. "Thank you."

Opening the containers, she made her selection and settled down on the other end of the sofa.

"Turns out there was an app on your phone tracking everything. The good news is that we now know how he was able to secure a date with you. Looks like it was on there before you filled out their survey."

Her heart sunk. "That means all my work stuff was seen, too." She swallowed. "Your stuff, too."

He brushed the thought off with a wave of his hand. "I have my DNA test done and results are back. At this point it would just be putting the truth out there. Even then, I never cared as much about what people might think as you did."

"It's my job," she reminded him.

"Still, it doesn't matter to me. The reputation I have is already far worse than a baby I didn't know about."

He had here there. "So now what?"

"Trying to figure out how the app was put on your phone. In the meantime, I got you a new one. Matt set it all up already and made sure it was secure. No extra apps." He handed her a phone. "I didn't take you for someone that played puzzle games on their phone."

She blushed. "Hush."

Taking the phone she unlocked it and went through the few apps she used the most, ignoring the unread messages she had. It was Monday and she really should have been working but with every-thing that had happened, she hadn't thought much about it.

"Guess I should answer some of these," she sighed.

"Or leave it until tomorrow. I don't think anything is world ending?"

"Can't say it's world ending, but I don't want things to pile up."

"Guess I should have held that until tomorrow then," he joked.

She snorted. "Probably."

Ryker stood and gathered all the containers, carrying them to the kitchen as she ate and responded to texts. The emails would wait until tomorrow.

She answered questions for most of her staff before finally setting the phone back down.

"Any update on the Luke front?" Catherine asked as he came back to the room.

"Nothing." Ryker shook his head. "His missing right now. It's more than just being with some woman or something because he goes completely dark. Even his phone doesn't travel with him."

She tapped her chin as she thought. "How long as he been gone?"

"Almost a full day," Ryker lamented. "If he sticks to his usual pattern, he should return early tomorrow morning."

"What's half a day away from here? That's the furthest he could go and get back, but we'd need to shave a little time off for doing whatever he is."

"Yeah, we're working on it. Problem is that it's a wide area and I can't think of what the little shit would be doing to even make a guess."

"I know it's wrong, but could we like track him somehow?" she hedged. It was wrong, but she was concerned, not just for herself but also for Luke who she feared was in over his head in something bad.

"I don't know what we could use, though. He's not taking his car. I don't even know how the hell he's getting there."

She thought on it for another moment. "What about his coat?" Catherine asked. "It's cold as hell out there right now and it'd be worth a shot."

Ryker nodded. "We can give it a try."

With a plan in place, she felt a little better. Maybe they'd reach the end of this sometime soon. Food forgotten, she stood and walked over to where Ryker was sitting, curling up beside him.

The TV played a movie that she hadn't even noticed was on but peace settled over her as his arm came around her, pulling her closer. She slept there until he carried her to bed, deeply and unaware of the danger that she was about to be in.

Chapter Sixteen
Ruker

By some miracle, Catherine had agreed to work from home today. Well, from his home, but he wasn't sure it wasn't hers now too.

It had only been a few days, and they had settled into a nice routine with each other. Catherine was feeling better than she had when the package arrived and overall was getting back to her normal self.

The night they shared hadn't been repeated yet, but he wasn't upset. Her sleeping against him, knowing she was there and safe, made everything right in his world. Not that he'd turn her down if she tried to start something.

She'd shocked him with her acceptance of his orders in the bedroom. He expected her to get angry or push back and when she didn't, he nearly lost himself before even touching her.

"Hey, Hacker Guy is on the phone," Catherine walked into his office.

Ryker rolled his eyes. "What's Matt want?"

"He was looking into a client for me, but had a hit on where

Marcus might have put the app on my phone." She put it on speaker and set the phone on his desk.

Ryker pulled her into his lap as Matt started talking.

"It looks like our guy was at a function with Catherine. I'm watching the footage now seeing when he picked up her phone, but that means it was on there much longer than we thought. This was six months ago."

"Was he just waiting on me to try the restaurant?" Catherine asked.

"I think he was waiting for any kind of in, that just happened to be it. Problem is, he's got someone else with tech skills helping him because there is no way he was able to do all of this on his own and make it work. Shit, there it is." Matt went silent.

"Send it over to us," Ryker told him.

"Doing it now," Matt said.

A moment later an email came through. Ryker opened the video on his desktop and dragged it to his monitor in the middle so they could both watch.

Marcus walked into the frame seconds after the clip started. Catherine was talking to someone, and he casually bumped into her, apologizing as he did. What most people wouldn't even notice was the sleight of hand that slid her phone from the blazer she was wearing.

"How did I not notice that?" Catherine gasped.

He held her tighter. "Most people wouldn't. Our guy is skilled at this."

"Can we not call him that?" She shuddered. "He's not our anything. Just a creep."

He nodded.

"Taking note. The suspect then takes the phone and carries it out of view of all the cameras before handing it to someone to give back to you," Matt explained. "I can't prove it, but I'd bet this is when he did it. Ryker I need that phone."

"You'll have it today," he promised. "The gift, too."

"Send it over asap."

The call ended, and Catherine looked up at him. "I don't even want to use my phone anymore."

He could understand that. She had been violated, digitally, but it was a violation. "This one's safe. We will make sure it never leaves your sight again."

She dropped her head on this shoulder, relaxing for a moment before standing. "It just really pisses me off."

"Completely reasonable reaction," he assured her.

"I hate this and I had that I still don't really know what's going on." She paced his office space. "I also hate that you have to have me here, I'm sure you want your space back and for me to go home."

Where did that come from? He wondered. "Cat, I don't want you to leave. In fact, I was going to ask you today if you wanted to set up some office space here so you don't have to use the sofa anymore." He hadn't known how to bring it up before, but now seemed like the right time.

"You don't mean that?" she questioned him.

He stood and went to her. "I absolutely do."

"What about when this is over?" she asked.

He took her hands in his and tilted her jaw up until she was looking at him. "We will figure that out then." Another thought occurred to him then. "Unless you want to leave?" His heart lept up to his throat as he waited for her to answer.

"I don't want to leave." She didn't specify if that was just now or ever, but he hoped it was ever because she'd quickly moved in and become everything. He couldn't imagine being here without her anymore.

As much as he wanted to tell her that now, he kept it to himself. She had enough going on already, he didn't want to add pressure of whatever they might be beyond the here and now on her.

"How much work do you have to do today?" he asked her.

"Only like four days worth," she laughed. "You?"

"The same." Dropping one of her hands, he led her out of the office and down the hall.

"Where are we going?" she asked from behind him.

"To destress," he told her.

"Destress, huh?" Her mood changed as they made it to the bedroom and he knew she was into what he had in mind.

They kissed, tongues meeting as they fell onto the bed, her under him. Ryker couldn't resist grinding against her. She made him needy, ready to take everything she was willing to give him.

Catherine broke the kiss. "We're a little overdressed for this."

He chuckled at her and pulled away to a stand. He undressed faster than he had in years, not having been so eager in any memory he could conjure up. Then quickly rolled on a condom, making a mental note to buy more because he was certain to run out of the few he carried regularly.

She undressed from her position on the bed. When she lifted her hips to shimmy off the leggings she had only put on an hour or so ago, Ryker couldn't help the growl that came from deep in his chest.

No sooner than they were both unclothed, did Ryker cover her again. Their lips met again, and he propped himself on one elbow, letting his other hand roam to tease her as he deepened the kiss.

Catherine moaned into his mouth and turned her head. "Take me," she begged.

"You want hard and fast?" Ryker needed to clarify before he did anything. He wanted hard and fast but if that wasn't what she wanted, he would happily take his time, too.

"Please, Ryker," she begged again.

He backed away. "Turn over," he demanded.

Quickly, she rolled to her stomach, lifting her ass in the air. He gave her no warning as he found her soaking wet already and drove home.

Home was what this was, too. It was like she was perfectly made for him and he fit like a glove inside her. He took a moment to savor the feeling of her wrapping around him before he pulled out and thrust again.

Making sure that Catherine was comfortable with this pace, he asked, "more?"

"Yes!" she cried out.

Needing no further motivation, Ryker set an intense pace for the both of them. He pulled out and thrust back in with a force that he was sure would send him over the edge in no time.

She gripped the bed and did her best to hold herself still. Ryker gripped her hips, moving her to the rhythm he was setting for them. Her moans filled the room as she chased her own release along with him.

It didn't take long before he was feeling her pulse around him. She squeezed him tightly as she came and cried out.

He kept up his thrusts and fell shortly after her with a shout of his own. Catherine's body went slack under him, her hips only raised due to his own grip on them.

Finishing, he pulled away and quickly disposed on the condom. She was on her back on the bed, smiling lazily at him when he returned.

Her flesh was red on her hips where he had gripped her. Immediately, guilt washed over him at leaving any mark on her. He had lost more control than he had intended if he was gripping her that hard.

"I'm sorry," he apologized, frozen just a step away from the bed.

Her brows drew together. "What for? That was amazing."

Closing the distance between them, he knelt on the mattress and traced the red marks on her hips. "That might bruise."

Her hand gripped his hand and pulled it to her lips. "First, I am not complaining. Second, I think this is exactly what we wanted, hard and fast. Marks happen, I'm glad to know they were because we were both so lost in the moment."

"I didn't mean to hurt you, though." Even as he settled next to her, he still felt unsure about it.

"Do you think I don't know that?" she asked. "Of course you

didn't mean to hurt me. I wanted this just as much, if not more than, you." She rolled onto her side to face him. "I liked it, Ryker. That's all that matters to me."

He didn't argue with her again about it and she relaxed into his shoulder. Holding her, he felt a little better but still regretted that he'd taken things too far in his mind, even if she was trying to convince him otherwise.

Another thing that alarmed him was how much concern he had over a handprint. She had clearly enjoyed it and he'd never cared before. With her, he wanted to take care of her more than himself.

As they lay there and Catherine quickly fell asleep, he analyzed over and over why it mattered so much with her. The trouble was that he knew why and it had probably always been the truth even when he was pushing her away. Maybe it was why he pushed her off before.

One thing was true, he knew he'd hurt her in some way, this just wasn't the way that he'd assumed it would happen. If they were going to continue whatever this was between them, he needed to get a grip on himself before they did that again.

Chapter Seventeen
Catherine

By the time Friday night rolled around and poker night for the guys was underway, Catherine's nerves were out of control. They were going to attempt to track Luke today and no one else in their friend group knew.

She and Ryker had agreed that they would let everyone know about the stalker, who hadn't bothered them since the package he left, but leave out what they knew about Luke like they had with Cade and April.

All the women had gathered at April's for the night to have their own party away from the men. Catherine had pushed not to have it be one group hangout as they often did anymore. She was nervous about what Luke would say or do and wanted to keep herself away from him as much as possible until they knew what was going on.

"You okay?" Kayla asked and set next to her on the sofa. "You're being very quiet."

Catherine shrugged, she hated lying to her friends. "Just still worried about this stalker guy and what he might do next."

"I'm so sorry about all of this. I don't know how we could have prevented it but I have my team looking into it. I know it was a one-off situation for now, but what if other people try it?" Kayla rambled.

"What are we talking about over here?" Lauren interrupted them.

"Why there's always something going on at Blind Date," Kayla sighed.

"It's not your fault," Catherine assured her friend. All the other drama has been her father's doing and somehow this was too.

"Where's your drink, girl?" Kayla asked standing to make sure Lauren got one.

"I'm not drinking tonight," she said quietly and dropped one hand to her stomach.

Catherine and Kayla gasped at the same time. "You're pregnant?" they squealed.

April arrived at that moment. "Lord, yes. So very pregnant. I'm tired, y'all. Don't mind me if I fall asleep."

"Not you," Kayla laughed. "Her." She pointed at Lauren.

"Really?" April's demeanor changed quickly from exhausted to excited.

Lauren nodded. "Jake is telling the guys tonight."

Hugs were shared by everyone as they congratulated her. Tears poured from April as she apologized for them and blamed her hormones.

"When are you due?" Catherine asked, doing math in her head, trying to decide how long she had to shop. They might not have been truly related, but they would all be aunts to any babies had by any of the women here tonight.

"It's still early, I'm only three months along." Lauren sighed and rested her hands on her stomach.

"You sneak!" April shouted in false annoyance. "You kept this to yourself for so long!"

"We wanted to make sure that there were no issues first."

"That makes so much sense. I was in a different situation," April hugged Lauren again.

April had needed to get pregnant to fulfill a contract that she'd made with Cade. They'd quickly moved on from their contract marriage to a real one, and gotten pregnant anyway, but it didn't change the circumstances of how everything started.

"I for one am I excited to be an aunt, twice," Kayla clapped. "Are you going to find out what you're having?"

Lauren shook her head. "We are going to let it be a surprise unless we need to know."

"Yes! I can start shopping now then," Catherine giggled.

The women chatted about all things babies for most of the night. It was hard to keep herself fully engaged in the conversation as thoughts of her own baby had crowded her mind for the first time.

She never thought of herself as particularly maternal but with two friends pregnant she was starting to wonder if maybe that was something she wanted. Or maybe it was her growing relationship with Ryker causing these thoughts.

It was definitely too soon for that conversation and she wasn't sure that Ryker would ever want kids. Then, he was trying to make sure this kid was taken care of even though it wasn't his, which was completely unexpected.

"Deep in thought there," Kayla nudged her. "Thinking of one of your own?"

Catherine immediately shook her head. "Of course not. I'm just thinking of what I want to buy for Lauren."

"It's okay. I'm thinking it, too," she admitted.

She sighed, caught. "It's too new for us to even talk about it. I don't know where this is coming from."

"Definitely all the hormones in this room and the lack of alcohol." Kayla winked. "I think you'll make a great mom when you decide to have one."

"Same to you," Catherine agreed.

Her phone chimed, and she turned it over to see a message from Ryker.

"How's that all going?" Kayla asked.

"Oddly smooth. I don't know why but I feel like I'm waiting for the bottom to fall out. What if this is him just being worried for me and when it's all done he changes his mind?"

"Sweetie," Lauren soothed. "I promise you that while he does help people more than he wants anyone to know, he never takes it so personally. Ryker hides from any chance of people thinking that he's not some big bad guy. You're personal for him, I wouldn't worry."

"Agreed," Kayla said. "Ryker wouldn't do this on a whim. He spent so long avoiding it because he was attracted to you. This just made him realize he needed to stop pretending he wasn't."

"Absolutely. He was just being stubborn and the chance that he might lose you completely by your dating and then the terrible guy from the date just made him wake up." April sunk onto the ottoman.

"Well, enough about me. Since everyone is getting pregnant, we need to change up what we do on girl's night. Definitely no more alcohol." Catherine held up her drink.

"Movie night?" Kayla offered. "We can watch the sappy romantic shit the guys don't want to watch."

"Yes," they all agreed.

Catherine grabbed her drink and took it to the sink. She took another sip before pouring it out. She was no longer in the mood for one and didn't want to drink by herself, anyway. Kayla was usually reserved in her drinking, so she wouldn't have more than one, anyway.

While everyone else was still in the living room, she took out her phone again and finally read the message from Ryker.

> Ryker: Luke is being quiet tonight.
>
> Ryker: Did you hear the news from Lauren?
>
> Catherine: I did! So excited for them.
>
> Ryker: I did the thing we wanted.

She knew he was talking about dropping a tracker in Luke's

jacket. There was actual fear in wondering where it would lead them that she had to swallow back.

Catherine: Okay.

Ryker: Anything strange happen?

Catherine: No. Is it weird that it makes me nervous that we haven't heard from him again?

Ryker: No.

Catherine: Thank you for expanding on that.

Ryker: You don't want me to. Make sure everything is locked up.

Catherine: It is.

Ryker: Good.

She wanted to tell him she missed him but that felt clingy. Instead the conversation had fizzled until it was bordering on awkward.

Ryker: Thinking of you in my bed.

The smile on her face almost hurt it was so wide. This was big from Ryker and she knew it. In her excitement, she nearly forgot to reply.

Catherine: I think that can be more than a thought some time.

Ryker: You think or you know?

Catherine: I know.

Ryker: Better start thinking of what you want now so you can tell me all about it when we get home.

That wasn't the first time this week that he'd called his house their home. Tonight she would not question it and just live in the moment and enjoy it. If it ended, then at least she didn't waste the time being unhappy.

Catherine: I can't think of anything else. Can't wait to be home with you.

Ryker: That could be arranged sooner rather than later.

Catherine: I think maybe we don't cry off too early. You're hanging out with my brother after all.

Ryker: If your brother knew what I was thinking about doing to you he wouldn't want me anywhere near him.

"What are you doing?" Lauren asked.

Catherine's face flamed. "Nothing."

"Oh, I love this for you. Is that Ryker?" She pointed at the phone.

"Yeah," Catherine admitted.

"I'm so happy that he's putting that smile on your face. You deserve to be this happy and giddy."

"Me? I'm so excited for you. You're having a baby." She hugged Lauren again.

"I still can't believe it."

"You better believe it, soon that baby won't be in there anymore."

"Write that man back and come join us." Lauren waved her away. "Be quick though, I think they're ready to start a movie."

Catherine smiled at how much their lives were changing. All of it was for the better and she was happy to be around for it and get to see everyone making great moves. It didn't hurt that she was getting her own happy right now.

> Catherine: I can't wait. I miss you already.

She fired the text off and quickly locked her phone back and tucked it in her pocket. She wasn't going to second guess it. It was sent and it would be what it was now. Hopefully, he didn't mind it.

Just as she joined them for the movie, her phone went off one more time. Her heart raced as she pulled it out, nervous about his reaction.

> Ryker: I miss you, too, Cat.

The smile that spread across her face had all of her friends gushing with her over Ryker. They called her out on it and the movie was forgotten, chatting instead.

Chapter Eighteen
Ryker

"What the hell?" Ryker stared at the message he just received from Matt and blinked, re-reading it again before calling Matt directly.

"I don't make the data, Ryker," Matt answered.

"Is this for real?" Ryker demanded.

"I don't play jokes, you know that. Besides what the hell point would that serve to send a joke about this and have you pissed at me?"

"Did you double-check?" Ryker ignored everything else.

"Is everything okay? You're yelling." Catherine came into his office.

He ignored her for the moment. "Check again," he demanded.

"I already checked it three times because it didn't make sense to me either. Right now I'm working on seeing if I can get into the video feeds and hear the conversation. I'll let you know if I do." Matt ended the call.

The thing that no one knew about Matt was that he was successful in his own right. He didn't need to cater to Ryker's attitude because he did this work, because he wanted to, not because he needed to. Ryker paid him more than well for his time, but Matt was a comfortable on his own, he didn't live paycheck to paycheck or even spend his money as far as Ryker could tell.

"What's happening?" Catherine asked.

"Come here," he said.

She walked over to him behind his desk. He pulled her down into his lap again where he preferred her to be. She was going to be upset when she got this information and he wanted to hold her.

"Read this." He pointed at the screen and the message he'd gotten from Matt.

"HG?" she asked. "You have him saved as Hacker Guy in your phone?" she laughed.

He didn't acknowledge it and waited for her to read the message. Her back went stiff, and she tried to pull away from him.

"Is this real?" she asked, her shocked voice a whisper.

"He assures me he checked it three times." Ryker held on to her, doing his best to comfort her.

"Call Cade," she finally said.

Ryker nodded and called Cade on his phone, putting it on speaker.

"What's up? I'm about to go into a meeting," Cade answered.

"You need to reschedule it. I'm calling a meeting at my house right now." They hadn't used it in a long time but they had a code to let the friend group know that something important was going down.

"Are you serious?" Cade asked.

"Seems to be the question of the day," Catherine answered. "You need to get here."

There was a pause before he spoke again. "Bring the girls?"

"Yes," Catherine said.

"No one is to tell Luke." Ryker hated it had come to this. "Not shitting you. Don't let him find out."

"Fuck," Cade swore. "I'll be there asap."

The call ended and Catherine stood to pace. "Why would Luke be visiting my father in jail?"

"I don't know," Ryker answered honestly.

He placed the calls to everyone else letting them know of the urgency and to keep it from Luke. It made him feel like shit to call a meeting to discuss Luke but everyone needed to be on the same page before they confronted him.

"I'm going to go make snacks," Catherine managed and then quickly left the room.

He fired off a few more messages to Matt before printing out the proof.

Ryker: I need this asap. I know you're working on it but I'm calling a meeting at my house.

HG: Do I need to be there?

Ryker: Not unless you get something else.

HG: I really am working on it. It's not the most secure thing I've hacked, but it's not the easiest either.

Ryker: Just hurry.

Catherine was in the kitchen spreading out what appeared to be everything from their fridge.

Their fridge? Another realization washed over him as he realized he had let her in and realized how easy and right it felt to have her here, but everything was now theirs and it had just happened.

"Do you think this is enough?" Catherine asked, pointing at the bar.

Ryker cleared his throat and pushed his thoughts away for later. "I think this is ridiculous, but if it makes you feel better to do it, it's more than enough."

She bit her lip and looked everything over. "You're right. It's too much." She started to reach for one of the plates she'd set out.

Ryker went to her and covered her hand, making her put the plate down again. "Cat, I know you're stressed, and it's okay. I don't know how this will end, but I can tell you it will be okay. We will get through this. Leave the food. It will get ate or we will put it away, either way it's fine."

"I don't know what to do," she turned and pressed her face into his chest. "I don't like not knowing what to do."

"I know, baby. I know." He stroked one hand up and down her back as they stood there.

It wasn't long until Evan and Kayla showed up. They had already been nearby and together when he called them.

"What's going on?" Evan demanded when Ryker let him in.

"You're the first to get here," Ryker said. "I don't want to go over it twice and I'm buying some time for Matt to get us more information."

"Who's Matt?" Kayla asked Evan.

"Hacker Guy," Evan answered.

"He has a name? I thought he was all incognito, and no one knew who he really was. Now I'm sad that there's no mystery there." She faked a pout.

They knew she was joking mostly, but her joke had served the purpose of breaking some of the tension in the room.

"I'm so hungry," Kayla sighed and joined Catherine in the kitchen. "Oh this is a lot of food. Are you okay?"

They were hugging when Evan and Ryker joined them. Everyone else trickled in with Cade and Lauren being the last to show up. With Lauren being Cade's assistant, they had ridden together.

Lauren went to Jake when they got there, sending questioning glances at everyone. "I told you we would be last to get here," she fussed at Cade.

Cade pulled April into his side. "Is Owen coming?"

"They're out of town," Ryker told him. "We can fill him in later."

"Then that's everyone. What's the big deal?"

Before Ryker could answer, someone knocked on his door, silencing everyone in the room.

"I swear if that's that Marcus dude, I'm going to fucking kill him." Ryker muttered as he went to the door.

Shock didn't cover what he was feeling when he made it to the door. The man in jeans and a hoodie stood there with a bag on one shoulder and his phone out in his other hand. Matt had shown up.

"Does this mean you have it?" Ryker demanded.

"Why else would I be here?" Matt answered, pushing his way past Ryker and into the house. "I'll set up in the living room."

"Who's that?" Lauren asked as Matt walked past, not acknowledging anyone.

"Matt," Ryker grunted.

"Wait, so he not only has a normal name, he's a real fucking person?" Kayla asked, surprising everyone.

Ryker shook his head at her and led everyone through to the living room. "I'll start explaining and then Matt can show us what he found out."

"I refuse to believe his name is Matt. Hacker Guy forever," Kayla declared.

Everyone laughed, even Matt who turned and winked at her.

"There are some things we left out of what we know about the person stalking me," Catherine started the explanation. "Luke was partying with him and apparently they had a disagreement, but Marcus won. We don't know what it was about. The reason we didn't tell you all is we wanted to see if it was even relevant and we didn't want Luke to know we were looking into him."

Cade's leg bounced a million miles an hour as Ryker recognized the man's struggle to stay calm. He took over their story from there.

"What we did know was that chunks of time was missing from Luke's life. Time where he didn't take his phone, his car, or anything identifiable or trackable with him." He left out that he was already having Luke investigated. "I slipped a tracker in his pocket at poker night."

"What the fuck?" Jake asked.

Ryker cleared his throat. "What I learned right before calling everyone is one of the places he was going."

"He was visiting our dad in jail," Catherine blurted out.

"I'm set up if y'all are ready," Matt added.

Silence filled the room as everyone processed Catherine's information.

"I was able to get audio and video of the most recent visit. I'm running to see when he was there and get the other ones."

"Play it." Cade was completely still, he'd lost most of his battle against the rage in him. April was holding his hand, probably the only thing keeping him grounded.

Everyone faced the TV as Matt pulled the video up. They watched as Luke walked in to the private area. A prisoner was escorted to a table in the center of the room and the guard left.

"I'm not doing this anymore," Luke said.

"Doing what?" the inmate asked.

"Anything for you. This is the last time I'm coming here and I'm not interfering with anything anymore." Luke stood near the door he'd come in from, not approaching the man.

"Then I'm not following through on my end. Your sister will be dropped from everything she's worked hard for because you don't have the weight to make it happen. Even from jail, I can have her removed from that school, and no other Ivy League will let her in."

Luke hesitated but pressed on. "She will understand."

"Will she?" he arched a brow and folded his hands over his round belly.

"Harvard," Matt added. "She's a senior."

"You're thinking you'll just make a big donation, right? No amount of money will save her from the disgrace of being thrown out when my friends and I support it," he threatened.

"No. She will figure it out and can go somewhere else. She's almost done anyway," Luke argued.

"Kid's negotiation tactics suck," Ryker commented.

"There will be nowhere else to go to get that degree, not after I'm done with her. She must have been sleeping with quite a few professors to be pulling that GPA," he said casually.

Luke's fists clenched at his side. "We will get through it."

"You won't have any friends left either, Luke. Once they figure out how you've been helping me, they'll drop you completely. You know they will. You were never close to any of them except Ryker anyway and he's fucking my daughter, so I can tell you where his loyalty will fall. You need to think this through before you ruin everything."

"I can't do it. That guy is into some weird shit and he's already ruined any chance with Catherine by stalking her. Not my fault he couldn't just be a normal person on a date." Luke tried to reason.

"Figure out something else. I need that merger to happen. Too much is riding on it."

"Why do you even care?" Luke shouted. "It's not like you can use anymore money from here."

"You'd be surprised."

Luke banged on the door he was standing next to.

"I'll see you next week, Luke."

The door opened and Luke rushed out of it without another word.

They watched the video until the inmate was taken away and then it cut off.

"That's all of it. From what I can tell, Luke was visiting once a week skipping very few. I assume he was meeting with him before he was in jail, but I don't have records yet." Matt typed on his laptop without looking up.

Everyone looked at each other as they all struggled to understand what happened. Luke was being bribed, and it made Ryker feel a little better about all this. At least he wasn't just setting them all up. He had a reason.

Chapter Nineteen
Catherine

"What do we do now?" Kayla was the first to ask. "Like, I hate that he's involved in any of this, but he's in a hard place, it seems."

Catherine agreed. "I don't know how I feel now. I was pissed, but now I don't know. Should we just confront him?"

"Like an intervention?" Lauren asked.

The guys stayed quiet. This was why these men needed their women. They were all probably ready to lose their shit and beat the kid up. Sympathy rushed through her as she thought about what was going to happen.

"Call him, tell him it's a meeting," Cade said to Ryker. "I think they have the right of it and I want to know how deep this goes."

"I can also add that the Marcus guy is just an idiot. The bear he sent wasn't even encrypted. He's watching a wall in the lost and found at the bus station now. Not even pretending to mask his IP." Matt looked up at the group. "I know I'm not really involved, but I think you guys should talk to your friend because he seems naive."

"Anything on Marcus's next move?" Ryker asked.

"Dude's a fucking weirdo. He's into some kinky anime shit and that seems to be all he does. He hasn't made any plans and if I had to guess, Luke is supposed to do something."

"Gross," Catherine made a face. "What's his business that I'm supposed to merge?"

"That's the thing. He doesn't have one. It's his father. What I can't figure out is what he's supposed to merge with? There's no business tied to your father anymore. Marcus's father owns a shipping company."

"Which one?" Ryker asked.

His tone had Catherine focusing on him instead of Matt's answers, waiting for his reaction.

"Paulson Holdings."

"Fuck," Ryker swore. "How much of Cade's company stock do they own, in percentages."

Matt typed away. "A cool 3%."

"Catherine, how much do you own?" Ryker asked.

"Eight," she answered.

"So combined that would give his father a seat on the board with ten percent," April added.

"I'll sell, right now," Catherine said. "Then there's nothing to gain."

"Likely the deal would still go through because the father must want the marriage."

"From everything I've learned about this guy, not even the most pressed women would bother to marry him for money. Catherine is his only hope at a marriage."

"Gross," Catherine sneered.

"Get Luke here," Cade demanded.

Ryker pulled out his phone and called him. Everyone in the room went quiet.

"Hey man," Luke answered. "I need to talk to you."

"Same. Calling a meeting at my house, it's urgent. Get here now," Ryker told him. It was the same way he told the other guys.

"Why?" Luke's tone held suspicion.

Ryker

"Not over the phone." Ryker ended the call and hoped it was enough.

"Should you have hung up on him?" April asked.

"That was normal for him. If he had stayed on the phone, it would have raised more suspicion from Luke," Evan explained.

"Now what?" Jake asked. "We just wait for him to get here?"

"I made snacks," Catherine said. "You too, Matt."

"Awe, did I lose the nickname?" Matt joked with Catherine.

"Well, now you're real. It's weird." Kayla said.

"I should have just emailed these over," Matt lamented.

"Wait, how did you get here so fast?" Catherine asked.

Matt winked. "I get to retain some mystery."

"Teleported," April stage whispered.

The women continued their teasing speculation as they left the living room.

* * *

Ryker waited for them to go before taking a seat. He needed a minute to absorb everything that they'd just learned.

"I know you like him, but he has to be honest with us. We can't help him if he hides things," Cade told him.

Ryker nodded and rubbed his temples. "I don't understand why he didn't come to one of us."

"He clearly was being manipulated. That doesn't make it okay, though."

"I know you never really liked him, Cade, but I've never misjudged someone so bad." Ryker stood and went to the window, looking out. "I brought him into our group, Cade. Now look at all he's done and is putting Catherine in danger."

"I'm pissed about that, too. Let's just see what he has to say."

Cade being the reasonable one about Luke was different. It only showed how strange things were right now.

"He's calling me," Ryker said, taking out his phone.

121

Cade nodded and waited for Ryker to answer.

"What?" he answered.

"I can't come right now. I have something I need to handle and it can't wait."

"What could possibly be that important? This can't wait, everyone else is on their way." He was trying to find a balance between anger and friendship.

"Ryker, I'll explain when I know more, but I have to go do this. It really can't wait."

"Luke," Ryker growled.

He didn't have time to say anything else because Luke ended the call.

"Matt," Cade called out. "Track Luke now."

Matt carried a plate filled with food back into the living room. "On it. He not coming?"

"Said he had something important he had to handle right now. I swear to God if he's going to talk to Marcus I am going to go throttle that kid myself." Ryker paced as he waited for more information.

Matt shared what he was doing on the large TV. "There he is."

"What the hell is he doing there?" Cade asked.

It was an apartment building in the lower end of the city. Definitely not one that any of them would frequent. He appeared to be standing in one of the apartments.

"Can we get a list—" Cade started before Matt cut him off.

"Here." Matt flashed a list of all the tenants on the screen.

They looked the list over. "Is that Paisley from the coffee shop?" Cade asked.

Matt typed some more. "It looks like she used to work at the one you frequent."

"I don't believe in coincidences," Cade said.

"Call everyone back in here. We need to figure this out." Ryker said. "Something else is going on. Dammit!" He resisted, barely, the urge to put his fist through his own wall. Every time they figured something out, they ended up with more questions.

They all piled back into the living room and Ryker decided that if they ever had to do this again, they needed a conference room. This was difficult to accommodate everyone for such a serious matter. He hated conference rooms, though.

"He's leaving." Matt pointed at the screen. "Looks like he was only there for maybe ten minutes."

"That's weird," Catherine said. "What would be doing in that area of town?"

"What's Paisley got to do with all of this?" April asked.

"She lives there," Ryker answered.

"Can't be a coincidence." Cade paced. "But none of it makes sense."

"I think that you're trying to force the pieces to fit. Paisley hasn't worked at the coffee shop for months. I can't see her having anything to do with Luke." Catherine's voice of reason had others nodding.

"Then what is it?" Cade shouted.

"I'm going through all the people in the building right now. It's going to take some time." Matt was steadily typing on his second laptop.

"How many computers did you bring?" Ryker asked.

"A few." Matt shrugged.

"Leave him alone so he can work," Cade pointed at Ryker. "What is he's there to meet someone to do something to Catherine?"

"Oh, so now it's not Paisley?" Kayla asked.

"Here's there for a reason. Call him again," Cade demanded.

Ryker took out his phone and called Luke. Straight to voicemail. "It's off."

"What are we going to do when we lose track of him? At some point he will take the jacket off." Kayla tapped her fingers on her leg as she asked. "I think we are all jumping to some seriously bad conclusions. We need to separate fact from assumption."

April stood. "That's a good idea. I wish we had a white board in here." She looked around for something to use.

Matt pulled a tablet out of his bag and did a few things on it before it appeared on his TV screen. He handed it to April. "You can use this."

She smiled at him. "This is great, thank you. I take it back, you are a real person."

He shook his head, smiling, and went back to his laptop.

It took half an hour but April had sorted everything they had discussed into two columns on the tablet. Ryker stood back and studied it, realizing what little they actually knew.

"I have a few shady characters that live there. Mind if I take over?" he asked April.

"Go for it." She handed him the tablet. "Can you email that to us?"

"Yup." He switched their view to his laptop and went over the people that lived there.

There were some felons and a few domestic violence charges on no less than four tenants, but nothing that stood out.

"What the hell was he doing there?" Ryker wondered out loud.

"Did you do a deeper dive on Paisley?" Cade asked.

Matt nodded. "She's in debt up to her eyeballs and has been to the doctor a lot lately, but there's been no big deposits to her accounts, no significant changes."

"I think we need to go have a visit with the old man," Cade said to his sister.

Catherine swallowed hard. "I don't know that we would get much."

"Anything is more than we have now," Cade argued.

"You don't have to if you don't want to," Ryker reminded her. "Cade can go alone or we can figure something else out."

She nodded, but the fear was clear. "I think I need to do this."

Chapter Twenty
Catherine

Catherine rode with Cade to the jail a few days later. Neither of them had spoken for the entire journey, both lost in their own thoughts. They were nearing the jail now and the tension in the car was increasing.

Ryker and April had both offered to come as moral support, but they had denied them. It had hurt Ryker that she didn't want him there, but she didn't know how else to handle this. With Ryker nearby, she might fall apart.

He was quickly becoming her rock and the one person she felt comfortable letting her guard down with. That meant that he saw a side of Catherine that no one other than Cade had ever seen. She needed to be strong for this, though. Needed to not have him waiting for her to collapse into when she left because she might not be able to hold it together.

Knowing he was home waiting on her was enough. She'd be able to hide everything until then and if she couldn't only Cade would know.

"So, you and Ryker, huh?" Cade broke the silence.

She groaned. "Now? This is the time you choose to do this?"

"I'm just wondering how serious it is between you two," Cade said as though it was a super casual thing.

She was wondering herself. "It's new, Cade."

"When you know, you know," he shrugged.

Catherine rolled her eyes. "Nope. You're so full of shit. You literally hid from April for years."

"Doesn't mean I didn't know."

"Whatever."

A few minutes later Cade pulled into the parking lot. "Are you ready for this?" he asked.

"Nope," she answered. "But I'm gonna do it."

"Same," Cade answered.

The process of getting in to see him was more difficult than she had expected. It was violating and intrusive and she felt gross. The first thing she was going to do when she got home was shower.

The guard, or the cop, maybe both? She didn't know. He led them to a waiting area and told them to have a seat. She and Cade looked at each other, debating it.

Neither of them felt comfortable sitting, so they stood near the wall and waited. The guard seemed not to want to leave them.

Another glance between them and they both sighed and took a seat. Catherine sat on the edge of the chair, not wanting to lean back. She was too nervous to sit back. The guard finally left them alone, and she hoped it was to get him so they could be done.

Nothing in her was able to pretend that this wasn't an awful experience. Her parents were in jail and she was here to see one of them.

"Do you know if we will be in the same room that Luke was?" she asked Cade.

"I have no idea how this really works." Cade shifted in his seat again.

"What are you going to say?" She hadn't worked it out yet.

Shrugging, Cade shifted again. "I figure I'll just ask what comes to mind."

"Follow me," the guard returned and snapped at them.

Catherine jumped out of her seat, literally, and struggled to take a breath. This was it. It was time to do this, and she hadn't wanted to back out as much as she did right now.

"If you want to go to the car and wait, you can," Cade gave her an out.

Catherine shook her head and steeled her spine. "I can do this."

It wouldn't have been so bad had he not literally held her and April against their wills. It wasn't like he was just in trouble for some white-collar crimes; this was actual craziness.

"I still can't believe he fought to be here instead of getting the help he needs." Catherine followed behind Cade, whispering.

"He has more freedom here. Visitors like Luke can come and see him and it's less monitored. I can't believe he won the fight."

She sighed. Cade was right and they should have maybe fought harder against it. At the time, she really believed that everything was over when he was convicted.

"Through there." The guard pointed at the open door. "No touching the inmate, no exchanging anything that wasn't already approved. If you want to leave before your time is up, knock on this door."

They walked through and the guard slammed the door closed behind them.

"I knew they wouldn't, but I still can't believe we are in here alone." Catherine looked around the gray room with the chairs and table bolted to the floor.

"They're recording, remember? Probably watching in real time but giving the false sense of privacy."

She nodded and bit her lip, waiting for the other door to open and their father to walk in.

After what felt like forever but was probably less than a minute, the other door unlocked and their father was led in. He was cuffed to the table and the guard then left through the same door, closing it firmly behind him.

"Ah, my children. To what do I owe this pleasure?" he asked, sounding cheerful.

"We want you to stop harassing us and our friends," Cade answered.

He laughed in answer. "I assure you that I am not doing anything. Just serving my time."

Catherine took a step forward. "So you aren't trying to get Marcus to marry me so you can have his father in your pocket?"

"What purpose would that serve?" he challenged.

"The seat at the board table. I know, and you know, that would give you strings to pull on Cade's company," Catherine spat back, waving her finger as she spoke.

Cade rested a hand on her shoulder, silently telling her to calm down.

Their father leaned forward and rested his elbows on the table. "You two must think pretty highly of me to think I could interfere with the company from in here. I would imagine the stories you make up and pretty wild.

"Knock it off," Cade warned. "We know what you're up to and we're done dealing with it. From here on out every time you think you can pull something over on us we will be there to stop it. This won't work and neither will anything else."

"If you keep it up, we'll take you back to court and have you committed for real this time." Catherine threw the threat out there, unsure if it would matter.

He threw his head back and laughed. "You can't prove any of these accusations, not legally." He looked up at the camera. "Let that be a lesson to you."

"You think so? These records can be subpoenaed and we have a damn good legal team. What do you think would happen if they blocked you from having visitors or phone calls while all this is tied up in court?" Cade stepped in front of Catherine. "We want to know what all you have in the works, now."

"Son, there's not a chance in hell that I would tell you anything even if your delusions were true. Maybe you have a little bit of crazy in you. I hear it's genetic." The casual way he spoke was doing its job and pissing them both off.

Cade's fists clenched at his sides. "I won't ask again. Give us what we want to know or we're leaving and my threats aren't empty."

"I'm afraid you'll have to see what you can do then because I don't know what you're talking about."

"Let's go," Cade said as he turned to Catherine. "This was a waste of time, just like the person over there."

"Careful now, I would hate for something to happen to either of you," their father said suddenly, menace is his tone.

Catherine's breath caught as he tossed out the warning.

Cade turned to face him which only caused their father to start laughing. It echoed in the empty room, sending shivers down her spine.

"That's enough, old man. You're a worthless piece of shit who will die in this jail with no power over anyone." Cade banged on the door to let the guard know they were done.

Catherine flew through it the moment it opened, eager to be away from him. That laugh would haunt her dreams, she knew it.

Getting out of the jail was much simpler than getting in, ironic. As soon as they were in the car, Cade locked the doors and took off.

"I'm going to call April," Cade told her.

The Bluetooth came on and dialed her number. She took the time to text Ryker and let him know they were done.

Ryker: How did it go?

Catherine: Awful and we didn't get any information.

Ryker: We knew that was a risk. Are you okay?

Catherine: No.

Ryker: What do you need?

Catherine: You.

Ryker: I'm here waiting for you.

Catherine swiped at a tear falling down her cheek as she read his response. Cade was just getting off the phone with April when he noticed.

"We won't be doing that again," he assured her.

Catherine nodded. She didn't think she could handle it again.

At one time, she had no real issues with her parents, but everything had changed in the last year or so. She constantly questioned if her father had changed or if she had just been blind.

Cade had never gotten along with him. They were like night and day, and even when she was little, she knew that.

"It's not our fault," Cade finally said. "That he's lost his mind, it's not because of us."

"How do we know we won't do that too?" She voiced her fears.

He gripped the steering wheel and glanced at her before returning his attention to the road. "We can't guarantee anything but I like to think that we are better people now than I ever remember him being."

Catherine let the truth of Cade's words wash over her. Neither of them were greedy or mean. Sure, she could be a bitch sometimes but usually because the other person was acting worse.

Maybe this wouldn't happen to them. Maybe they wouldn't change.

Chapter Twenty-One
Ryker

"Can I still call you Hacker Guy?" Catherine asked Matt as they sat in the conference room in Cade's office.

"Stop flirting with him and get over here," Ryker pulled her away from Matt.

"I'm just asking a question. I didn't know him in real life when he got that nickname."

"He didn't need it then or now," he bit out.

Catherine laughed.

It had been two days since she and Cade had gone to visit their father and everyone was meeting again to come up with another strategy. It hadn't given them anything.

"Has anyone heard from Luke?" Ryker asked everyone.

They all shook their heads, looking at each other.

"Dammit." Ryker was worried about him and didn't have a clue how to help.

"He went home yesterday," Matt said. "Hasn't left since."

"You're just now telling me?" Ryker shouted.

"You're just now asking. It wasn't anything out of character, so I didn't see the need to bring it up."

"We need to talk to him." Ryker clenched and unclenched his fists. "This is important."

"Like I said, he hasn't left."

"Can we get back to the task at hand?" April intervened.

Catherine came over and slid her hand into his, holding him steady as he worked through his anger and next steps.

"Okay, the plan is to gather everything that we legally can and see if it's enough to prove guilt of something on Marcus. Though, if I find something bad, even illegally, I'm not above an anonymous tip to the proper authorities." Matt spun in his chair to face Ryker. "It's not going to be as easy as we want it to be."

Ryker nodded. "Nothing ever is."

"And if it is, it's a trap," Matt finished the quote. "So, going back to April's list, we want to cross out what we know is true but we can't legally prove. I also pulled up a list of all his known associates and if anyone knows them, because y'all are connected somehow, then you're going to see what they know."

"If we start asking around about him, won't that tip him off?" Catherine asked.

"Doesn't matter if it does. He should know by now we are on to him. Or he's just that dumb, either way, it won't matter." Matt ran a hand through his short brown hair.

Catherine made a small "hmm" sound, indicating she wasn't sure she believed him.

Ryker walked to the window and looked out into his backyard. He wanted this settled and for Catherine to have peace over all of this. A small part of him wondered if they should get married and maybe that would stop her father's pushes.

Marriage? Where had that come from? They hadn't even discussed her staying with him beyond this situation resolving and now he was thinking about marriage. Hell, she was the only woman he'd ever let in his house for any reason, he was definitely getting too far ahead.

The thought of Catherine not staying with him after everything was over was jolting. He didn't want that to happen, but he didn't know how to stop it. If she wanted to leave, then it was her choice and he wouldn't beg her to stay.

"Ryker." Catherine placed her hand on his shoulder. "You good?"

He nodded and cleared his throat. "Just thinking about what we need to do still."

Catherine gave him her own nod and walked back to the sofa. He'd probably upset her and now that would be another thing he'd have to deal with.

If she left, those moments would happen less. He wouldn't need to feel like he was going to cause a fight for being himself in his own home. Then, he didn't feel that now most of the time. Catherine wasn't clingy, and she didn't get upset when he got broody.

"Okay," Matt said loudly. "I've sent the list of known associates to everyone's emails. Go through and start there." He was good at giving directions Ryker noted. There might be another business for him to create if Matt was interested.

The topic of business pulled him out of his thoughts of Catherine and what came next. Tossing those ideas around in his head, he pulled out his phone.

Skipping the email that Matt had sent to everyone, he opened a note and typed in his ideas. He wanted to get those down before he lost them. It would be a good business and he'd take Matt on as a full partner if he was interested.

"I know a few people," Cade said.

"Same," Jake agreed.

"Unfortunately, I don't know anyone," April admitted

"I'm pretty sure a few of these are clients at the restaurant." Kayla reached for a notepad from the stack they had sitting on the table and began to write.

"Good," Ryker joined the conversation.

"I know you know a few, so I think you, Cade, Jake, and I should divide and concur," Evan was already writing in his own notepad.

Catherine was quiet but was looking at the list. Ryker joined her at the table, taking a seat next to her.

"Do you know anyone?" he asked softly.

"Not many and none I would feel comfortable asking any questions. A few passing acquaintances are on here though." She worried her bottom lip and continued to look at the screen.

Ryker reached up and released that lip from her teeth. "It's going to be okay," he assured her, hoping he was telling the truth, and that she believed him.

"Ryker, make your list," Evan said.

He grunted his annoyance to Evan, but pulled the list up finally. There were more than a few names on there that he recognized. None that he had any close relationship with, thankfully.

He wrote up his own list and handed it to Evan to do whatever he was going to do. If Ryker had to guess, there would be a spreadsheet before too long, probably color-coded and he'd be assigned people to contact.

"From here, we need to make sure we are staying in contact with Matt who will hold all our evidence. I don't think anyone really knows how closely involved he is with this so he's the best person to keep it together."

Matt agreed. "I can also dig a little deeper on what you find out to confirm or deny it."

"Thanks for all your help with this," Catherine told him sincerely. "I don't know where we'd be without you."

"I want to go try to speak with Luke," Ryker said. "Anyone opposed?"

"You're not going alone," Cade told him. "I have a few questions myself."

"I think we should all go. Minus the ladies, sorry." Jake turned to Lauren. "We don't know what kind of state he's in and I don't want any of you getting hurt.

Catherine nodded, quickly agreeing not to go. The other women followed shortly after and Ryker breathed a sigh of relief that they wouldn't have to argue about this.

"We can go now while you keep working with Matt." He turned and kissed Catherine.

"Please be careful," she whispered. "I don't know what I'd do if something happened to you, especially if it was because of me."

"I don't think Luke will hurt us," Ryker told her.

There was no way of knowing, though. People that you thought were great could turn on you in a second when backed into a corner. He'd seen it often and had even used it to his advantage in business.

"We will keep in contact with you," Evan promised Kayla.

"I have the feed in his building accessed. There're no cameras in Luke's apartment, but I can at least track the movements of every-one," Matt added. "What if things go wrong?"

Leave it Matt to be the one thinking of the contingency plan. Ryker didn't want to think of anything going wrong to the point of needing a backup plan but it was for the best. "If something goes absolutely sideways, call the police."

"Agreed. We can leave you out of it but I think we need to get the authorities involved if Luke gets violent. I doubt it will come to that." Jake pushed his chair back and stood. "I'm ready when you are."

They all kissed their women and left them sitting at the table to go confront the person they had once considered a friend. There wasn't far to go as Luke enjoyed staying uptown and near the nightlife.

"What do we think he's doing?" Evan asked as Cade drove them to Luke's building.

"I think he's just lying low and trying to figure a way out of his own mess," Jake answered. "I don't see him doing this without the coercion so I'm not even sure how to deal with this."

"We will figure it out when we talk to him," Ryker said. There was no good end to speculating.

They all grunted and settled back in their seats. There was too much to consider to know where to go. Winging it was their only option.

As the car pulled up in front of the building, Cade slowed and turned into the valet lane. They all got out, probably looking like a clown car with all four of them climbing out.

Nothing was said as they got in the elevator and rode their way up to the top floor. Luke's apartment wasn't somewhere they'd been often. Ryker had been there the most and even those times had been rare.

The doors opened and Ryker led the way to Luke's door, banging on it like a cop when he got there.

"Who is it?" A female voice called out.

Shocked, Ryker turned to his friends who all shook their heads, they didn't recognize the voice either.

"It's Ryker. I need to talk to Luke," he figured it was best to just go ahead and be honest.

The door opened and a blonde woman, strikingly similar looking to Luke opened it. She sent him a questioning look.

"Is Luke home?" Ryker asked.

"I don't know where he is," the woman answered. "He's talked about you before, but we've never met. I'm Ashley, Luke's sister." She didn't stick her hand out to shake, just stood with the door half open and her blocking the entrance.

"When was the last time you talked to him?" Ryker pressed.

"Just a few days ago. He told me that something was going wrong, and he needed to handle it. I haven't been able to reach him since and I came here yesterday hoping to figure out what was going on. What do you know?"

"We are trying to figure that out, too," Jake said with a smile. "Can we come in?"

"Who are you?" she asked.

Ryker introduced everyone, and she opened the door wide. "He's talked about all of you."

"Have you figured anything out?" Ryker asked as he walked in.

"No. I was looking for information on you today, actually. I was hoping you knew something."

Ryker made eye contact with Cade and let him take over from here.

"Your brother is being blackmailed, and it has to do with you. We don't know anything more than that and he was supposed to come by the other day and then bailed on it." Cade studied her as he spoke. "Has he talked about anyone else?"

Tears welled in her eyes. "No. Mostly him and sometimes your names were mentioned. He didn't really talk to me that often, just said he was busy with work."

"What work does he do?" Jake asked.

"He just told me it was boring, and he didn't want to talk to me about work. I didn't push him. I suppose that was selfish of me. I was just happy to have some money and be able to go to school. Do you think it was something illegal?"

Ryker looked for any sign that she was lying but came up with nothing. "His business wasn't illegal that I know of. He made most of his money with stocks, though. There's no way to know if he was getting inside information."

"Do you mind if we look around?" Cade asked.

"Go for it. Let me know if you find anything." Ashley waved her hand and gestured to the entire apartment. "I've already looked."

The men separated and began a search. After an hour, no one had found anything, and they all joined Ashley back in the living room.

"How long are you going to be here?" Ryker asked her.

She shrugged. "I don't know. I'm worried about him, but I need to get back for my classes."

"Do you have a number we can contact you on if we find something out?" Evan asked.

She recited her number. "You will let me know if you find him, right? Even if it's not good?"

Ryker assured her they would, and they left. There was nothing there, but the fact that he was out of touch with his sister was a big deal. What else could he have been involved in?

They all brooded in their own thoughts and after explaining everything to the women, they went their separate ways to get more information on Marcus. Matt volunteered to monitor Ashley to make sure that nothing Catherine's father had threatened Luke with actually happened.

Ryker disagreed with telling her the whole story and won the argument. There was no need to scare her since they didn't have solid proof of what Luke was doing.

Chapter Twenty-Two
Catherine

Ryker was putting dinner in the oven the next night when Catherine joined him. He was surprising her tonight with a meal that he was making from scratch.

People assumed that because he had money he didn't know how to do anything basic like cooking. He told her earlier that he'd had to cook a lot for his mom and him if they wanted to eat when he was growing up so he knew how to make a few meals., but it seemed she had underestimated him.

"I have a question," she said as she wrapped her hands around the back of his neck. "What's happening with your court case?"

"I actually got an email today that her attorney is requesting a second DNA test through a company of their choice."

Catherine wrinkled her nose. "What is that going to prove? They can't seriously think you faked a DNA test. You had the results sent directly to both sets of lawyers, right?" This whole case seemed so strange.

Ryker nodded. "My lawyers are pissed. I told them to figure it out, it's what they get paid to do."

"Hmm. Can we figure out what she wants?" Catherine dropped

her arms and drummed her fingertips on the counter as she thought. "There has to be an endgame here. She wouldn't be doing it for no reason."

"I'm letting the lawyers figure it out. I have enough to figure out with Marcus and Luke."

"What are you cooking?" Catherine asked, changing the subject.

"Baked chicken," he answered. "Potatoes and broccoli to go with it."

Catherine's jaw dropped before she quickly recovered. "Culinary skills, huh?" This was a step up from the other night. More work, in her opinion.

Ryker just grinned at her.

"I can't wait," she assured him and lifted on her tiptoes to kiss his cheek.

The doorbell rang and Ryker tensed. "Any chance you'll actually stay here?" he asked her.

Catherine shook her head.

"Fine. Stay behind me, then." Ryker stepped in front of her.

She followed close behind him, but made sure to keep Ryker between her and the door. Hopefully, it was just one of the other guys and this was nothing, but she didn't have high hopes considering everything else happening lately. Odds weren't in her favor.

"It's Marcus," Ryker whispered to Catherine. "You need to leave," he said through the door.

"I'm not leaving. You are holding my future wife hostage and I'm here to help her break free of you." Marcus shouted.

His words were clear, and he didn't sound drunk or anything. What had driven him to come here now was all she could wonder.

"I am not being held hostage. Leave me alone," Catherine shouted as Ryker glared at her.

"Prove it," Marcus snapped.

"No," Ryker shouted. "You have one minute to get out of here or I'm calling the police."

"If you call the police, then you'll be in trouble, too. You know they're looking for you and they'll see that Catherine is being held and arrest you for that, too."

"Looking for me?" Ryker whispered.

"Open the door!" Marcus shouted.

Catherine backed up. "Open it so he can see I don't want to leave with him."

"No. It's not safe," Ryker argued.

"Fine," she sighed. "Hello? Police? I have a stalker that won't leave my front porch at this address." She wasn't on the phone, but she hoped he would take the hint and see she was serious.

"Don't listen to the things he's telling you. Just wait until the real truth comes out!" Marcus shouted and rapped the door with his fist three more times before leaving.

They waited for him to leave, checked the cameras and went back to the kitchen.

"Stay with me," Ryker said. "I don't trust that he's really gone."

"Me either," Catherine admitted. She was concerned that when he saw no police show up, he was going to come back.

They sat down to their meal not long after Marcus left, both trying to put away the events of the day. Neither of them spoke about it and the tension was clear between them.

Dinner was good, and she was surprised by the well seasoned and perfectly cooked chicken. She didn't tell him she was worried it wouldn't be good.

"Thank you for dinner," she told him as they got ready for bed.

"You don't have to thank me," Ryker told her. "We nothing needed to eat."

She noted he was uncomfortable with the praise and left it alone. It was cute, she thought, that he didn't want to be acknowledged for cooking dinner.

"You ready for bed?" Ryker asked.

It was getting late, and she had just been thinking of that herself. "I'm actually exhausted. I'll be happy when all of this is settled and I don't have panic moments in the middle of every day."

"I'm sorry that it's not over yet." Ryker followed behind her up the stairs,

"It's not your fault. It's my father, again. I just hate that he's still able to do this to me after I thought it would all be over."

"I know, baby." He pulled her in for a hug before stepping back.

They both went through the motions of getting ready for bed, quietly together. It was strange to stand in the bathroom and brush her teeth alongside him but she liked the company.

They'd gone from zero to one hundred in their relationship quickly, and every time she thought about it, she got butterflies in her stomach. She didn't want to leave him when this was over.

As they slid into bed, Ryker stretched his arm out to her so she could curl up into his side. They didn't talk anymore, and she slowly drifted to that space in your mind that's between awake and asleep.

The sound of shattering glass had her sitting straight up in the bed. Ryker was on his feet before she could blink.

"Stay here. Lock the door and call the police," Ryker told her as he opened his bedside drawer and pulled out a gun. He checked it and she heard a click before he started towards the door.

Catherine jumped out of bed behind him and locked the door. She ran back for the table on her side of the bed and snatched her phone off it. As the light from the phone filled the room, she dialed the police and went to the bathroom to hide, locking that door, too.

She could hear things breaking downstairs and her hand holding the phone shook as the phone rang.

"I need police to my house. Someone broke in and my boyfriend went downstairs," she cried in a whisper.

"Police are on the way," the dispatcher told her after getting some more information.

She told them that Ryker had taken his gun with him and the dispatcher had asked a few more questions that Catherine struggled to answer through her tears and her focus on the noise downstairs.

A gun fired and she couldn't stifle her scream. "A gun went off," she told the dispatcher. "Please hurry."

She prayed it wasn't Ryker that had been shot as she listened to the dispatcher try to calm her down. Not long after, flashing blue lights filled the room.

"The police are here," Catherine said.

"Stay where you are, ma'am. They will come to you when the situation is under control."

Catherine nodded, not even considering that they couldn't see her. She listened as voices filtered through the floor. She couldn't tell what was being said, but it didn't seem frenzied.

"Ma'am?" the dispatched asked.

"I'm here," she answered.

"Can you unlock the door to the bedroom? The police are there and you can come out now."

"Okay." Catherine stood on trembling legs and unlocked the bathroom door, stepping into the bedroom. She sucked in a breath before going to the bedroom door and opening it.

An officer stood on the other side, waiting for her.

"Do you see the police?" the dispatched asked.

"They're—they're here."

"Okay. You can end the call now."

Catherine brought the phone away from her ear. The officer motioned for her to follow him.

"You're going to go downstairs and straight out the front door, okay? Another officer will meet you and guide you to a place you can be warm while we determine what happened here," he explained.

"I know what happened. Someone broke into our house," she told him.

"Thank you," he said, brushing her off.

"Can I call my brother?" she asked.

"The other officer will help you with anything you need." He guided her out the door and she spun on him.

"Where's Ryker?" she demanded.

"Ma'am, you need to step outside and we will explain everything when we can."

"Is he okay?" she shouted at him.

"He is alive," the officer answered.

She wanted to push back more, but decided not to cause any problems. She believed it would all work out. It had to. They had done nothing wrong. She would be with him soon.

"Miss?" the other officer greeted her. "Come with me, please," he guided her away from the house and into a waiting SUV where she was instructed to sit and wait.

Chapter Twenty-Three
Ryker

"I told you I don't know what you're talking about," Ryker snarled.

The police had taken him from his home in the back of a police car down to the station. Ryker was pissed, they wouldn't let him talk to Catherine or reassure her that all would be fine. He now knew why.

"Sir, it seems strange to us that the man you shot and killed is the same man that was helping the woman that is accusing you of forcing her and creating a child in the process." A detective sat across from him in the small interrogation room.

"I already told you I don't know her and that kid isn't mine. We had a DNA test done, and it proves that. I've never met that woman before."

"You have to see where we are seeing this from," the detective explained.

"No. I don't. He broke into my house. I was in bed when he did, you can ask Catherine." Shouting wasn't solving anything, but he didn't have it in him not to.

"A lot of things are damaged in the house. You said yourself that she was asleep. How would she be able to tell us where you were?"

"When she woke up, she saw me. I got pants on, grabbed my gun, and told her to lock the door and call the police. If I was going to do something wrong on purpose, why would I have her call the cops?"

"To make your case of self defense and I'm not buying it."

Ryker blew out a breath. "I want a lawyer."

"Only guilty people need lawyers to talk to the police," he said, standing. "I'll be sure to let you know when they arrive."

Ryker slammed his fist on the table and let out a roar in his frustration. He didn't understand half of what they were talking about, all he knew was they thought he had intentionally killed Marcus.

It wasn't unintentional, but neither was it planned. Marcus had busted a window downstairs and climbed into Ryker's house. When they'd heard it, Ryker had gone down to confront the intruder with his gun.

Marcus had been waiting for him and had pushed him when he reached the bottom of the stairs. They had fought and struggled for a minute, and eventually, Ryker was able to get his gun aimed and shoot Marcus.

He maybe should have aimed less lethally, but the man was fighting him. What did Marcus have to do with the DNA test woman? He couldn't even remember her name and he'd already proven the child wasn't his.

Five minutes after the detective left, Ryker's lawyers were walking in, making demands as they did. He needed to give them all a raise to deal with this.

"If you aren't charging our client, then you need to let him go. He's done with this interrogation." Charles was his lead lawyer on his cases and was quickly putting on a display as to why he was good at his job.

"Charges for the murder are pending. In the meantime, charges for rape have already been approved and your client is under arrest." The detective smirked at the lawyer like he'd won a battle.

Ryker

"Where is the basis of that?" Charles demanded. "We have not been notified of an investigation and have already submitted DNA tests to the court."

"That part's not my call and you know it. You'll have to wait for a hearing to have that argument with the judge," the detective explained. "Stand up," he told Ryker.

In quick order, the detective read Ryker his rights, cuffed him, and led him to a waiting cell. His lawyers argued the entire time before telling Ryker they would see him in the morning.

Ryker was shoved into the cell, uncuffed and ignored. He didn't know what time it was or when he'd get let back out.

He did his best to lay back and pretend to be unbothered but it didn't work. All hope of sleep was gone. He worried for Catherine and what they must be telling her was going on and what she might believe.

"If you want to talk, you let me know," the detective said as he walked by Ryker's cell.

Ryker didn't say a word as he stared the man down. He'd been arrested before and knew already that trying to talk your way out of things wasn't something that usually worked. That and they would spin everything against him.

For the first time in his life, he was fully taking his lawyer's advice and keeping his mouth shut. He was worried about doing it, but he couldn't see how talking earlier had helped. The detective had already decided on his guilt and that was unlikely to change.

"Your lawyers are sending over evidence from tonight's crimes that we can pretend will help you. We both know it won't," he rambled on. "In the meantime, welcome home. Even if you get yourself off this murder charges, we both know you can't get yourself off the other ones. Perverts like you deserve to be here."

The detective then spit at Ryker before finally walking away. Of all the places he imagined he might end up at, back in jail wasn't one of them.

This wasn't a simple petty larceny charge or a fight like the other times, either. No, this was more than that and he was starting to question how we would prove his innocence.

As was normal for him lately, his thoughts drifted back to Catherine. This sort of thing against him was exactly the like what he wanted to shield her from. He never should have let things go as far as the did with her. Now that he had, he didn't know what he was going to do without her.

He wouldn't blame her for going to her own home and staying away from him after this. He had killed someone and there was no taking that back.

"Ryker?" Catherine's soft voice said from the other side of the cell doors.

"Catherine?" He jumped up.

It was like his thoughts of her had conjured her because she was really standing there.

"You should be here," he bit out.

"Ryker," she started. "Don't do this. Don't be that guy."

"What guy?"

"The one that pushes the girl away while he's in trouble. We aren't going to do that. This isn't going away because it will all end soon." Catherine gripped the bars of the cell.

"Maybe it's because I need you to be safe and has little to with me. Get out of here because it's certainly not safe here."

"No. I'm not leaving yet. I came to check on you." She leaned forward and squinted. "Is your lip bleeding?"

He didn't know or care. "It doesn't matter. Go home and get your brother and get things sorted. You shouldn't be in here for any reason at all, least of all me."

Like he was drawn to her through a magnetic pull, Ryker still rose and went to her. His hands covered hers and he took in her tear-stained face and pajamas.

"Please, go home," he pleaded.

"This is going to be okay. We are going to do everything we can to make sure that you are home soon," she promised. "I needed to see that you were okay. I was so scared when the gun went off that you were hurt." Fresh tears streamed down her cheeks.

"I'm unharmed," he told her. He was far from okay. Confused, pissed, but not okay.

"You will be out soon. All of this is made up and I don't know what Marcus had to do with it and Hacker Guy is digging into this angle now."

He nodded and dropped his hands from hers. "Go home, please?"

Catherine nodded and walked away. She looked back at him twice on her way out and Ryker nearly told her he loved her. He did love her, he realized.

The realization shook him to the core, and he fell back onto the makeshift bed he had in this cell. He would get out, he vowed, and then he would tell her. Here wasn't the place, anyway. The last thing he wanted was to have this place be somewhere he remembered forever because of that. He'd prefer to forget that he was ever here.

He thought over everything that had happened and wondered when this woman had started accusing him of forcing himself on her. He hadn't. He didn't know her and he would never do that to anyone. Everything was such a fucking mess.

Instead of raging like he wanted to, Ryker sat back on the bed in his cell. Bed wasn't the right word for it. It was closer to a cot, but either way it was uncomfortable. There was nothing he could do now but wait and hope that everyone was able to figure this out. Between his friends and his lawyers, he at least had hope.

Chapter Twenty-Four
Catherine

Catherine had stayed with Cade and April, again, until Ryker's house was no longer a crime scene and was cleaned. It had been a few days already and Ryker had still been in jail.

She was in touch with his lawyers constantly and they were working hard, with Matt, to prove that all these charges were fake. She knew without a doubt that her father was behind this. There was no other reason for it.

"Any news?" April asked.

"Nothing." Catherine stared at her phone, willing it to give her something, good news of any kind would be welcome.

"He'll get out of this." April hugged her.

Catherine just nodded and swallowed back the tears that were threatening to spill over again. It seemed all she had done since Ryker's arrest was cry.

"I'm going to run pick us up some dinner and I'll be back, okay?" April grabbed her keys.

"You know we could just order delivery," Catherine reminded her.

"Believe me when I say I mean no offense to you, but if I don't get out of this house for at least five freaking minutes, I will lose my mind," she groaned.

Catherine laughed. "Better do it now, soon that baby will be here."

"That's another reason," she laughed. "Though I imagine that when that time comes it will feel a little different."

"Be careful," Catherine told her friend.

April nodded and left. She wouldn't be gone long but Catherine understood the need to leave. She also understood that she wasn't the problem, yet for the second time in a year she was living with them again.

She could have gone back to her house, next door to Ryker, but she hadn't yet. It didn't feel like home anymore. She'd spent more time at Ryker's since she bought that house and she wanted to go back there.

Settling down at the bar, Catherine casually munching on some popcorn as she scrolled her email. One particular email had come through about an hour ago and had her clicking on it.

Catherine-

I heard about your recent troubles and I wanted to extend my sincerest condolences on your poor choice in men. You never were good at that.

There is still an option of making everything right with me which might even help Ryker. I understand that Marcus is no longer with us but I do have another friend with a son who would be willing to merge with our family despite the mess you've put us in.

I cannot begin to imagine what you must be going through with knowing the man you have chosen to shack up with is really the lowest of the low, forcing himself on women. I can assume that may be what happened with you, and perhaps with some therapy, you will realize that.

The offer stands if you wish to take advantage of it and I will help with your friend's problems. Do let me know at your earliest convenience.

-Your loving father

Catherine screamed in sheer frustration. It was a good thing that no one was here but her. She called Cade immediately.

"Everything okay?" he answered.

"No, but I'm not hurt. Father sent me an email." She shook her fist and for the first time understood why some men would punch inanimate objects because if she was sure she wouldn't damage her hand, she'd happily hit a wall now.

"What the fuck? What does it say?"

"He all but admits he is the reason that Ryker is in trouble. Told me that I can create a merger with another person he knows and he will help with the legal troubles." She went back to the email and forwarded it to Cade and Matt. "I sent it to you."

"Give me a second." He was quiet for a moment. "Are you kidding me right now? How is he even emailing you, much less pulling all these strings? As soon as we get Ryker out of jail, I'm putting all the legal teams on Father."

"How do we prove it?" Catherine asked. She was ready to march up to the jail now and demand Ryker's release over it.

"We don't. The email doesn't claim responsibility. We know him, so we see it."

"Now what?"

"Nothing really changes. Send it over to his lawyers in case they can do anything with it."

She quickly did. "Should I reply?"

"Absolutely not. You won't be agreeing to do what he wants so there's nothing to say."

"Okay. I'll let you go. If I hear anything else, I'll let you know."

"I'll be home in the next few hours. I've got to catch up on things since I've missed so much and I want to take some time off when April has the baby."

"I love that you guys are so cute together." She ended the call and went back to her emails.

There was one other email that caught her attention. The sender was Danielle Wadson, the woman at the heart of all the allegations against Ryker.

Catherine-

You don't know me, but you should know of me. I have information for you and would like to meet asap. Please let me know when and where.

-Danielle

Before doing anything with the message, she scrolled the rest of her emails, making sure no more surprises were waiting for her. Satisfied that this was the only one, she forwarded it to Matt, Cade, and the lawyers.

Cade: Don't meet her.

Catherine: I'm calling the lawyers to see if we can all meet there.

Cade: That better be the only way you meet her.

Catherine: I'll keep you posted.

She dialed Charles's number and waited for him answer.

"Catherine," he answered. "How can I help you?"

"I sent you an email."

"I haven't had a chance to check it. I'll look now." He was quiet for a moment as she assumed he pulled it up. "Well, this is interesting."

"Something like that. I want to meet her. I was thinking that we could do it at your office with supervision?" Catherine explained she didn't want to meet the woman alone, but thought the information she could give them could help.

"I agree. It would certainly be a useful conversation to have. If she's willing to testify to anything, it would help a lot."

"Is there a time I should tell her?" she asked.

"Whenever you're both available. I will work around her schedule."

"Thank you. I'll let you know what she says."

"Please do. And call me, I will answer and I may not see an email right away."

"Thanks," Catherine answered before they ended the call.

Danielle-

I do know of you, though I don't think we've ever met. I would be happy to meet if you think you have something that will help Ryker. We can meet tonight at his lawyer's office.

-Catherine

She hit send and walked away from her laptop before she ended up in a vicious cycle of refreshing and waiting. The cycle was pacing and looking at the laptop, moving the cursor so it didn't go to sleep, and then doing it again.

April got home, and she explained everything that had happened in the short time she was gone while they unpacked takeout.

"I wasn't gone long," April said. "I'm sorry you were home alone, sweetie." April had taken to calling her that since she started staying here. It was probably the hormones, but Catherine wondered if it would stick past her having the baby.

Catherine checked her email again and held her breath as she looked at the reply. "She wrote me back," she told April.

"Open it," April scooted next to her so they could both look at the screen.

Catherine-

I can meet you there in the morning at 9. I'm done playing these games and I will tell you everything. I have to bring my child with me, sorry about that. Please know that I was doing what I thought was best here, but it's gone too far.

-Danielle

"This is it!" April squealed. "This will be the thing we need to get Ryker to come home."

Catherine prayed it was as she called Charles to tell him about tomorrow. He agreed with the time and let her know he would be there. It felt like the end of this was close, but she was scared to hope.

The only good thing so far was that the media hadn't picked up on it and with any luck at all they wouldn't. She could do damage control, but she didn't want to have to.

"I told Cade," April said.

"Thank you. He said he would be a few more hours."

"Yeah, he told me too. He might want to go with you tomorrow."

"He's welcome to since it involves our father in one way or another."

"I think I'll sit this one out."

They carried their takeout to the living room and got comfortable. April put on a movie and they sat quietly. Catherine couldn't focus on the TV but she did her best. Although she didn't want to get too excited about tomorrow, her heart felt light, hope was blooming.

Chapter Twenty-Five
Ryker

Ryker was given clothes to wear to court by his lawyer and was allowed to change. After, he was quickly handcuffed again and led out into the courtroom. It killed him for Catherine to see him this way.

She smiled at him, looking excited, and he hoped that meant they had a way out of this for him. He couldn't wait to see and talk to her again.

The judge called his case, and the lawyers began their arguing. Ryker focused on it as much as he could but there was a lot of legal speak that made it hard to keep up.

"Your honor, the accuser would like to speak today," Charles said.

There was arguing from the other lawyer but eventually, a woman was led to the stand and sworn in. After all the basic questions like her name, Charles asked her if she had ever met Ryker.

"No, I have not."

"Have you ever willingly or unwillingly had sex with the accused?"

"No, I have not."

"Can you explain to the court why you accused him of forcing himself on you?"

"I was bribed by the child's father."

"The child's father is not the accused?"

"He is not the father, that's correct."

"Who is the child's father?"

"Marcus Brockenson."

"And how did Marcus bribe you?"

"After I got pregnant, Marcus wanted nothing to do with me or the child. A month ago he showed up at my house and threatened to take me to court for custody of our child if I didn't do what he wanted. I couldn't afford to go to court with him so I did not feel like I had a choice."

"And what did he ask you to do in exchange for not taking you to court for custody?" Charles pressed.

"He wanted to me to accuse Ryker of being my child's father. I tried to explain to him that it wouldn't work. A DNA test would be all it took to prove he wasn't. He argued that this needed to be done so other things would work."

"What other things?"

"He never said."

"Why tell the truth now?"

"I was already planning to and then Marcus died. I no longer have to worry about what he will do."

"Do you have any proof of these requests?"

"I have text messages, yes."

"Is there anything else you would like to tell the court?"

"I'm sorry for all of this. I didn't feel like I had a choice. I was scared."

"Thank you. That is all."

The prosecution lawyer stood. "In light of this new information, your honor, the state would like to withdraw all charges against the defendant."

"I think that's the best course of action," she agreed. "Young lady,

I suggest you think more on the choices you make and how you could have ruined someone else's life before doing anything else."

Danielle nodded.

The rest of what happened was a blur. Things were said and Ryker's handcuffs were removed.

Catherine was there directly behind him and he turned, pulling her into a hug. He shook Charles's hand when he released her.

"Come on. Let's go do all the paperwork so you can go home." Charles pulled him away from Catherine.

He went and signed the paperwork. Charles would pick up his belongings from the jail, which wasn't much and his gun was being returned to him because they had already declined to prosecute the murder of Marcus.

Charles explained that there had been a video of him coming through Catherine's backyard into his. Then it showed him breaking the window. There was no video of what happened inside but there was too much evidence of a clear break-in to charge him.

"Catherine is waiting for you out front when we are done. Your house is no longer a crime scene and I believe she had a cleaning crew in there for hours yesterday, so you should be good to go home."

"Thank you," Ryker patted him on the back.

"Thank your girl. She was the one that got most of the work moving in the right direction. I've been a lawyer for a long time, so believe me when I say she's a keeper. Very few people have someone willing to fight that hard for them." Charles walked him out.

He planned to hold her tight as long as she would have him. He still killed someone, and that part was a fact. It all came down to if Catherine could live with that knowledge. Something like murder could really change her perception of him.

As they walked to the front of the courthouse, Ryker saw Cade and April. He looked around for Catherine, not spotting her. His heart sank.

"She said she would be up here," Charles said as they made their way towards Cade.

"It's okay," Ryker told him.

"Congratulations, man." Cade slapped him on the back. "I was really worried about you there for a minute. Should have known it would all work out."

Ryker continued to scan the crowd of people for Catherine.

"She'll be out in a minute. Said she had to talk to someone."

He nodded. He couldn't imagine who she would be talking to instead of out here, but he was happy she hadn't left.

They stood there chatting and waiting until he caught sight of her stepping out of a side room. She looked nervous but broke out into a huge smile when she saw him.

Catherine sprinted across the space between them as Ryker braced to catch her. She was in his arms for a few seconds, wrapping her arms and legs around him as she kissed him.

"I'm so happy that's over," she said, resting her head on his shoulder as she lowered her legs. "I wore pants today specifically to do that."

Ryker laughed. "I'm glad you thought it through."

"All right, guys. Let's get out of here. Your car is waiting." Charles pointed to the exit.

"I hired one just so we could talk," Catherine explained.

It worked for him. He had no plans to remove his hands from her for a long time if she let him.

He held her hand as they walked out the front of the courthouse and opened the door to the waiting car. They both waved at Cade and April before getting in.

Catherine slid over further than he wanted her to and he pulled her back into the middle of the car so she was flush up against him.

"I missed you," he whispered against her ear.

She sighed into him. "I missed you, too."

"Tell me what you've been up to," he said, curious as to how what happened today came about.

"Believe it or not, she reached out to me. It was all really strange that day. My father threatened me to leave you behind basically, and he would make it all stop if I did what he asked. Then she emailed and wanted to meet. We agreed to meet at Charles's office, and she told us everything. It was really sad."

"I don't understand what the point was still. Like, why were they doing this?" Ryker puzzled.

"It was supposed to make me not trust you. When it didn't work, they upped the game and added the new accusations. From what we could tell, Marcus grew impatient on the charges to come through and took matters into his own hands."

Ryker nodded. It made sense but only served to show how little Mr. Hawkins knew any of them. Catherine was fiercely loyal to her friends and would never have believed the allegations.

"From what we know, she wasn't aware that Marcus had passed until after she emailed me. His father hadn't informed her, and she wasn't a next of kin or anything. So she was never going to go through with it."

"I can understand her motives. I hate it. But I see why she was doing it."

"The sweetest little baby. I got to meet them both at Charles's office yesterday."

"Who were you meeting with after court?" He couldn't resist the question. It had to have been important if she wasn't out there. "Her?"

"No." Catherine worried her lip again.

Ryker tilted her chin up to him so they could make eye contact. "You can tell me anything."

"I saw Luke in the crowd. He looked a mess, and he didn't think anyone would recognize him. I pulled him to the side in the crowd and spoke to him privately."

Ryker clenched his fists. "What did he have to say?"

"He claims he was there to make sure that nothing went through, said he had proof that he was going to provide if he had to."

He grunted. Seemed awfully convenient since it worked out in Ryker's favor.

"Luke also said that he's working on some things to make everything make sense but he needs proof first. After that, he will be in touch with you first."

"Do you believe him?" Catherine was a pretty good judge of character from what he'd seen.

She nodded. "I think he's trying to get himself out of the mess without relying on you guys. He seemed unsure about if you or anyone else would be talking to him after he explained, anyway. Honestly, he seemed scared."

"He should just reach out to us then. We can help whatever it is and then get him back to right. Even if we don't all stay friends, we wouldn't abandon him." Luke should know that by now.

"If you think about it, he has no reason to think otherwise. He's never been as close with anyone other than you, mostly because he was too wild and careless. I wonder now if that was really who he was or if he was pretending some."

He kissed the top of her head. "A problem for another day. I want to go home, shower, and then get in bed with you."

Catherine giggled. "I think that's a good idea. I've missed you."

Chapter Twenty-Six
Catherine

Catherine ordered them some dinner while Ryker cleaned up. He explained he felt gross and she couldn't imagine what it must be like.

Her plan was to make everything as easy as possible over the next few days for both of them. The house had been cleaned and repaired, takeout was always a food option, and she didn't want to go anywhere if it wasn't necessary.

She was curled on the sofa as usual when Ryker came back down.

"Anything I should know about the repairs or that couldn't be replaced?" Ryker asked, still toweling his hair.

"No. Everything that was broken was replaced and the window. You'll need to go through your insurance for reimbursement since I'm not on it. I paid for everything to get done, though. I wanted you to be able to come home when this was over."

He nodded and sat next to her. "I wanted to talk to you about something."

Her nerves ratcheted up as what he could want ran through her head. If he asked her to leave, she was going to cry, but she'd go.

"I want you to move in, officially," Ryker rushed out. "You've been living here for a few weeks now and I don't want you to go. I know it's fast but I think that we could make it work. If you're concerned over the other night, I can promise you that I've never done that before and, with luck, won't need to do it again. I would if I had to. Protecting you, us, will always be a priority."

Catherine held her breath. She was surprised by what he'd hurriedly said and it took her a moment to fully process it. "Yes," she finally said. "Yes, I want to move in with you, officially."

Ryker's smile, rare though it was, split his face. "Yeah?"

"Yeah," she confirmed.

"We can look for a new place if you want," he told her. "Somewhere without the memories."

"I like this house," she told him. "If you want to move, we can, but I don't need to."

That night had been terrifying, but she was shielded from the sights of Marcus and the destruction that the fight had caused. Having not seen it, she was comfortable to stay where they were.

"Even with what I did?" he asked hesitantly.

Catherine rose up on her knees and faced him. She brought both hands up to cup his face when she answered. "You did what you had to, and that probably saved us both from something worse happening." She took a deep breath and said what she'd been holding back for a few days after she realized it. "I love you, Ryker. I don't want to leave your side."

"You stole my thunder," he chided. "I love you, too. I planned to tell you a bit later."

She threw he arms around him as she laughed.

Dinner arrived not long later, and they quickly ate and headed upstairs. Ryker led her to the bed and eased her down.

"Not hard and fast this time," he told her.

No, that wouldn't be what either of them needed, she agreed. She would have kissed him in response with words caught in her throat, but he was standing, instead she nodded.

Ryker laid down with her then, holding his wait on his elbows and kissed her. Slowly between broken kisses, they managed to undress each other.

He pulled away long enough to roll on a condom and was back on her. She knew without a doubt that tonight was going to change her, change them. This was intense, and they had done nothing yet.

She shifted on the bed, letting him know she was ready, raising herself up to meet his waiting cock.

Ryker hissed in a breath and lowered his mouth to hers. Their tongues danced and still he kept himself away from her.

When he pulled away again, she was about to complain, but his movements stopped her. He poised himself at her entrance and looked at her, holding her gaze to his as he slowly filled her.

It was the most wonderfully intense thing she had ever experienced. He held them there, him fully inside, stretching her, as he looked into her eyes.

"I love you," he said.

A tear slid down her face as she spoke. "I love you, too."

The intensity only built as Ryker set a slow and steady pace. She reached for her climax, finding it just in reach as he once again kissed her. It was somehow both too much and not enough.

One more deep thrust and Catherine lost it. She sailed over the edge, seeing stars as she did. Crying out against his mouth until he backed away.

Ryker wasn't far behind her as he roared his own release before collapsing on his side, keeping his weight off her. They were both breathing heavily as if a marathon had been run, and it was amazing.

He stood and disposed of the condom before returning to her. "That was... wow."

Catherine curled into her side, happy to have him back and the safe feeling of being in his arms. "It was."

No more words were needed. They laid there, wrapped in each other's arms until their breathing grew slow and steady, falling asleep surrounded by love and happiness.

Chapter Twenty-Seven
Ryker

Peace was a funny thing. Every time you thought you had it, you would lose it in the blink of an eye. It was like that for Ryker when he got out of jail and it seemed like everything was behind them.

Sure there was always the looming threat that her father would find some new way to scheme and plot against them, but they were working on that. They were also still looking for Luke.

Catherine had been the only one to have any contact with him and that was now two weeks ago at the courthouse. Matt had found that Luke was exploiting the camera systems in his building, looping it once when he left, and had timed it perfectly.

The only one he didn't loop was the lobby, but he didn't leave through it, so it didn't matter. Ashley had been staying at his apartment, hoping he'd come back home, but nothing so far. He also hadn't returned to the building that Paisley lived in which left them with even more questions.

Ryker had peace in some areas but without answers from Luke, knowing the kid was okay, he knew that peace was fleeting. There was still more to be done, and it wasn't over. He wondered if it ever really would be.

He pressed the elevator call button and waited for it to open. Today he planned to talk to Matt about his new business idea and hoped he was on board. If he had to, he would find someone else, but he wanted Matt to take it on.

The doors opened and Ryker stepped in, grateful to have it to himself. It gave him a few more moments to decide how to tell Matt the plan. By the time he reached Matt's floor, he had decided that direct was still the best approach, he'd lay it all out there and see what happened.

"Matt," Ryker called when walked into his office.

"Yeah?" he answered. "I don't have anything new in the last hour."

Now that the pressure was off them for the moment, Ryker hadn't been pushing for updates as often on Luke. He would surface again and Catherine believed it, so they had looked but not with any urgency.

"I had an idea I wanted to run by you," Ryker said as he pulled up a chair beside Matt's desk.

That got his full attention, and he looked away from his computer at Ryker. "What?" he said skeptically.

"It would be a lot of work, but one that would make you a lot of money if you're interested in heading it. I want to start a sort of security firm. But not just home security, which we'd have to do, but more personal security. If someone came to us in trouble like Catherine was, we would have men to protect the client in person and digital digging and surveillance like you do."

Matt stayed quiet, thinking it over. Ryker hoped he was on board with the idea because it would be profitable, but he wanted Matt to run the day-to-day. He didn't start new businesses or take them over without a plan for someone to run it.

"What if they can't pay us?" Matt asked.

"What do you mean?"

"Say someone comes to us and they need help, but they can't pay us. Would we do any cases like that?" Matt clarified. "Like not all the cases, of course, but would we turn them away immediately?"

Ryker thought about it. It had been an unexpected question, but one he was willing to answer. "I suppose not. There's no reason why we couldn't help someone in need here and there without payment. Especially if this takes off, we would have the funding to do it." He paused for a second and then asked his thoughts out loud. "Did you have someone in mind already?"

Matt shook his head. "No. Not yet anyway. There might be someone that needs my help soon, but it's not to that point yet. She's not in any danger at the moment."

Ryker smirked. Of course, it was a woman. "Well, if she reaches that point, we will help her. No payment required."

"Then I'm in." Matt held out a hand for Ryker to shake.

"I need to resource people and put it all together. Do you know anyone?" he asked.

"There are a few guys I served with that might be good on the physical protection side of things. I can put out a few feelers and see if anyone is interested."

Ryker gave him a curt nod. "Let me know if I can do anything on that front. I want to be clear, I would finance this, and I'll help some, but my goal is always to be hands off in the businesses I own. This would be your project."

"Understood," Matt agreed.

"Good. I'll have legal send you a new contract and this would come with a pay raise, too. All the details we can go over." Ryker stood and lid the chair back to where it belonged. "Another thing, we can't run it from here so we would need to come up with a new set of offices."

Matt smiled. "I know just the place. You want it to stay in town, right?"

Ryker shrugged. "I own businesses globally so I don't care where it's located but it would need to be somewhere near enough that clients would be able to come and meet us if needed."

"Not really, everything is online anymore. Those few dedicated people that would need a face-to-face before would just fly to us or us to them."

"Why don't you send me your ideas and we can meet about this again next week?" Ryker turned to leave.

"Thanks, boss," Matt said with sincerity.

Ryker nodded as he walked away. He thought this was going to be a venture that he could be proud of. It had been a while since he started from scratch on a company and was itching to get into the details.

He'd run the idea by Catherine tonight and see if she had any ideas on it and then the guys tomorrow at poker night. Starting new was exhilarating, and he found himself smiling as he stepped into the elevator.

Read on for a free book, Owen, the starter to this series and to order Luke's story!

Keep In Touch with Toni Denise

Follow Toni Denise on Social Media!
Facebook
Instagram
Twitter
And Sign up for her Newsletter to find out about awesome games
and new releases.
Sign up here!

Owen

Don't miss the prequel novella, Owen's story.

Owen is a man who always knows and gets what he wants, but when he goes to the bar to grab a nightcap, he gets more than he bargained for. He meets a woman who's unlike any he's ever known but saying goodbye to bachelorhood will take some convincing.

Jenna isn't thrilled with the idea of going on a blind date, but a deal is a deal, so she shows up. She meets a great guy, who saves her from what would've been a disastrous date. Unfortunately, she never hears from him again.

Even though, the unplanned date goes well, Owen has a big decision to make. Is Jenna the one who will make him rethink bachelorhood?

Find out what happens in the prequel novella to the Billionaire Blind Date Series!

To read the full story, sign up for my newsletter!
www.tonidenisebooks.com

Owen Chapter One

Owen stepped into The Striped Keg bar and looked around. The dim lighting was a stark contrast to the well-lit street he had just come in from.

Men and women chatted throughout the room, most standing at tables with a few lining the bar. He came here specifically to avoid too much conversation. Plus, as it was across town, no one recognized him.

They could if they looked hard enough, but few ever did, and that was what he wanted. A drink and some peace.

Walking around the old wooden bar, he took a seat at the far end and waited for the bartender to notice him. It had been a disastrous week, one he'd like to forget, and here where he blended in, it helped.

"What can I get ya?" the bartender asked.

He handed over his card. "Start a tab. I have a ride home, didn't drive here. Scotch."

He always made it a point to let the bartender know he wasn't driving. It helped make sure he wasn't cut off before he was done for the night.

"All right." With a curt nod the bartender walked away.

"Excuse me?" A pretty blonde in a black dress approached him. "Are you Kyle?"

Owen shook his head.

"Damn. Mind if I sit here?" she asked as she set her small purse on the bar and sat down without waiting for an answer. "Why I let my sister set me up on some stupid blind date with a guy name Kyle of all things, I'll never know. Then he's not even here on time? Way to set the tone."

As much as he didn't want to be, he had to admit he was intrigued by the plain-speaking woman next to him. She didn't even seem to care if anyone was listening to her monologue, just kept on going.

The bartender brought Owen's drink over and turned to the woman.

"A beer, please. Whatever's on tap is fine."

"Add it to my tab," Owen said without thinking.

It was stupid. She was going to sit here now and keep talking to him and there went all hope for his night of peace.

"You don't have to do that," she told him as the bartender walked away.

"Looks like you could use a good break tonight, figured maybe it would cheer you up."

"I'm not going to sleep with you," she said boldly, causing Owen to choke on his first sip.

"What?"

"Just because you bought me a drink and my date didn't show, I'm not so grateful that I'll drop my panties for you tonight. I don't do one-night stands."

Owen couldn't hold back the bark of laughter that spilled out. "You're very blunt," he told her.

"No sense in not saying what you mean here in a dark bar with strangers. If you want, I can pay for my drink myself when he comes back with it."

"It's okay. I don't mind paying for it with nothing in return." He flashed his most charming smile at her. "I didn't intend to get anything for it as it was."

"Thank you."

Her drink showed up a moment later and he let the bartender know she was on his tab until he closed out.

"Why'd you think I was your date?"

"Wishful thinking, perhaps?" She shook her head at herself before turning back to him. "You were late getting here and your tie is the right color."

"My tie?" It was a light green, one he wore often, favoring the color.

"Yeah, he's supposed to be wearing a green tie. That's vague enough, but what shade of green? There's so many, and then so many men in here with green ties."

He nodded as he listened to her ramble on about ties. She was animated when she talked, and he found himself enjoying it and her company. Normally he carried the conversations but didn't feel the need to with her.

"Sorry," she said suddenly.

"For what?" He tilted his head, trying to figure out what happened.

"I always talk too much. It's a fault of mine and annoys people." She sipped her beer as though that was making it all better because she couldn't talk.

"Oddly enough, I was enjoying your speech on ties and the various colors of green."

"Liar," she said but then grinned up at him.

"I am in a position where I don't want to be the only one talking but I seem to always be doing just that. Having someone I don't need to pretend I want to do all the talking with is refreshing."

"Well, flattery will get you everywhere," she laughed. "Except my bed."

"Got it. Not sleeping together tonight."

She shook her head but laughed.

"Excuse me, are you Jenna?" A man in a poor-fitting suit stood next to her.

Still facing him, he could see the indecision on her face as she looked back at who had to be Kyle. He looked like a jerk and was definitely older than both of them.

Finally, she answered, "I am. Are you Kyle?"

He nodded and then didn't even bother to hide it as he checked her out from head to toe. "Must be my lucky night. You are stunning."

Owen rolled his eyes and sipped his scotch. This guy was going to get nowhere with her and he was interested in watching it happen.

"Sorry, if you were looking for a hookup, let me save you the time. I won't be sleeping with you for at least a few months, if you last that long."

Thank God he had already swallowed his drink or he would have choked on it again. Owen let a small smile sneak out as he watched Kyle try to decide what to say to that.

"Months?" Kyle asked, the shock evident on his face.

"At least three, maybe six," Jenna confirmed.

"Umm, well, I," Kyle stammered and pulled at his collar.

Taking pity on him, Owen jumped into the conversation. "Dude, just cut your losses and find a new bar and date."

Kyle seemed to just register his presence as his gaze slid to Owen. "I mean, it's not that we had to tonight, but like, that's a long time."

Owen just shook his head. "Go on."

Kyle seemed slightly relieved as he spun and disappeared into the crowded bar.

"You really should have let him sweat it out a bit longer."

"Couldn't. The man looked like he was going to pop before he ever managed a sentence."

"A pity he was only looking to get laid. I'm never letting my sister set me up again. Where'd she even meet him?"

Owen laughed. "He looks like a used car salesman, and not a very good one."

Jenna threw her head back and laughed. "God, yes. That's exactly it."

"Months, huh?' Owen arched an eyebrow at her.

"For him? Absolutely. If ever." She looked at her phone. "He's almost an hour late and was clearly checking me out before he decided if he wanted to have the date. It's going to be a no, bud."

"Bud?" Owen teased.

"He looks like he calls people bud."

He agreed and nodded. The man one hundred percent looked like he did. "Well, now that you have no date tonight, what are you going to do?"

"You're not my date?" Jenna fake pouted before giggling. "Don't look so horrified. I'm not trying to trap you."

"Not horrified, more curious," he answered simply. "So what was supposed to happen on this date?" Curious now, he found he wanted to keep the conversation going and know more about her.

"I assumed we'd chat over drinks and decide if we wanted a second date. Didn't really think about it that deep to be honest."

"What a crummy date," Owen said.

"I agree. I really should have just stayed home."

"Now, that I wouldn't have agreed with."

Just then Kyle walked by again. "Months," he muttered, shaking his head before turning into the crowd again.

"Dude's a creep," Owen observed. "Want to get out of here?" he asked her.

Jenna pinned him with a look that had him backpedaling.

"To get pizza. I swear. It's walking distance, too."

She stared at him for a moment, and he knew she was deciding whether to believe him or not before she nodded.

"Bartender!" Owen called. "I think we're ready to pay." So much for the tab he'd been planning to run up.

Liked it? Get it for free by signing up for my newsletter at www.tonidenisebooks.com

Coming Next

Check out the next book in the series
Luke

Also by Toni Denise

Learn More or get buy links for any of these books at my author website:

tonidenisebooks.com

Westbeach Series:

Old Friends

On the Run

One Last Chance

Out of Time

Series Boxset

Finding Love Series:

Engaged to Her Neighbor

Married to the Playboy

Falling for Her Fake Husband

Short and Steamy Duet:

The Wedding Date

The Wedding Ruse

Stone Twins Duet:

Please Stay

Don't Leave

Billionaire Blind Dates:

Owen (free with newsletter sign-up)

Jake

Evan

Cade

Ryker

Luke

Stand-alone:

Fighting Chance

Bonus Content Old Friends

Sometimes a second chance can be the last chance.

Recently divorced, Kelly finds herself back in her hometown. Deciding that starting over is key, she and her son take to living a new life.

When a second chance with Mason, an old flame, ignites, Kelly is excited to feel love again.

But something is wrong. Someone is watching them, waiting to strike. Someone that knows them. Someone. . . close.

Not knowing who she can trust, Kelly is thrust into a life of fear and looking over her shoulder.

Where do you turn when the one person you thought you could trust might actually be the person you're running from?

A steamy romance novel with a moderate heat level, free on all platforms!

Old Friends Chapter One

Taking in the scenery, Kelly wondered why she never came back to visit. Going home was hard, but it was only about a four-hour drive. She really should have come home before now. Taking the long road around the outside of town, the scenery alternated between trees so dense the automatic headlights came on in her car and open pastures with cows or horses in them. This time of year, everything was still bright green. It looked pretty, but she knew better; being late August, it was hot out there. Soon the brilliant green would give way to a wonder of colors as fall slowly crept in.

Turning the music down, she focused on the GPS and the last few miles of her trip. Traffic had started to pick up in the previous hour of her journey until she left the interstate. She was glad she had left earlier in the day; it was only about 4:00 p.m. now. A quick check of the back seat showed Hunter was waking up. For a seven-year-old, he wasn't a bad road-trip partner, but he had slept all but the first hour, when he ate most of the snacks. "Hey, Hunt, we're almost there. Are you excited?"

"Are we in a zoo?" Hunter sleepily asked.

Kelly took another look around, wondering why this was even a question. Cows. There were cows on both sides of the road. "No, baby, there are ranches around here that raise cows."

"So, I'll see the zoo every day?"

"Yes." Simpler to agree than to explain more as he wasn't awake yet. Besides, in all his seven years, he'd never seen the countryside, and Westbeach was about as opposite of DC as you could get.

As they made the last turn, the woods on either side were a welcome presence, adding shade to the last bit of the trip, which had been mostly on the sunny highway. She was going to have a sunglasses tan for sure. Finally pulling in to the driveway, Kelly breathed a sigh of relief to see her aunt and uncle already there and waiting for them.

The light blue house was one level and had a small new porch on the front. The wood was still white looking, so she could tell it hadn't been there long. The front yard was freshly cut, and there were trees on both sides of the property and behind it. A privacy fence, which also looked new, wrapped around the backyard. No neighbors could be seen unless you were in the road. *Wonder if I'll be able to sleep without the noise of the city?*

Aunt Mary was the first to come off the porch as Kelly parked the car. Mary, in her signature flower dress and floppy hat over her white hair, had always been able to style anything except herself. Her dresses were like something older ladies probably wore in the fifties. Gardening, cooking, shopping—same dresses; some things never changed. Bob, on the other hand, was a jeans and T-shirt man. Kelly could never remember Uncle Bob having hair—on his head or face. Much like Mary though, his style was the same no matter what he was doing. The only thing these two changed was the colors each day.

When Kelly stepped out of her car, Aunt Mary immediately wrapped her in a welcoming hug. "How are you doin', dear? How was the trip?"

"Let her get out of the car, Mary." Uncle Bob always sounded a tad sour but was a sweetheart underneath.

"I am, I am." Aunt Mary backed up and opened the back door for

Hunter to climb out of the car. "Hunter! You've gotten so big!" Hunter grinned and stood tall at her praise. Mary ruffled his hair and proceeded to go to the trunk with Uncle Bob to get their bags. "Is this all you brought, honey?"

"For now. The rest is packed, and Dylan is supposed to send it this week, but we'll see if he remembers to let the movers in or not."

"Okay, let us know if you forgot anything." Aunt Mary smiled sadly at Kelly.

"You know I will." She plastered on a big smile to reassure everyone that she really was okay. Taking Hunter's hand, she turned and walked into the house.

When she walked in, the first thing she noticed was that the house was fully furnished; some things even looked new. A gray sofa in the living room faced a flat-screen TV with a small coffee table. Passing through the living room to the kitchen, she noticed there was a cherry-colored table for four with a bouquet of fresh flowers waiting for them. *Definitely Aunt Mary's idea.* And the smell—some version of every spice, but in a good way—was just like Bob and Mary's house. It was a welcoming scent, the smell of home.

Kelly walked down the hall of the modest one-story house, pulling her suitcase behind her. Three rooms, two bathrooms—per Mary's directions, hers was the last on the left. The room had a large queen-sized bed in the center with a gorgeous purple quilt and matching pillows on it. A dresser sat against the long wall with a mirror attached.

Checking all the doors, she discovered the closet was behind the open bedroom door, and against the wall was a master bath. A purple shower curtain hung already with silver bath mats. Aunt Mary really should have been an interior designer, and her remembering Kelly's favorite color just made it that much better.

Kelly had never been able to have everything decorated in her favorite color before, but now she could do her thing. Putting her bag down she took a deep breath; divorce wasn't going to be too bad if this was how it started. Coming back home wasn't all that bad, even if it did make her feel a little like a failure for her marriage not working.

There was no love lost in her marriage anyway. Dylan didn't even fight for custody of Hunter. He just let them go and agreed to everything—not that she had asked for much, just child support and custody. Dylan didn't even want weekends with Hunter. Kelly sighed as she looked in the mirror and pulled her hair into a ponytail before heading back out to the other three noisily chatting about cows in the dining room.

"Hunter tells me he's excited to see the zoo every day," Uncle Bob informed her with a laugh as he pulled Kelly up for a quick hug. Although pushing seventy, Bob was still a tall man. He was the exact opposite of Mary, who was shorter than Kelly by five inches, standing at five feet tall. The family had always joked that it was her hat that gave her an inch or two and that she genuinely was less than five feet. Mary had always laughed along as well, shushing everyone, but never argued it.

"Something tells me he'll eventually tire of it," Kelly said with a small laugh of her own.

"I stocked some essentials in the cabinets and fridge; wasn't sure what all you would need. We can go to dinner later, or you can come over and I'll cook." Aunt Mary always made sure everyone had eaten. If you weren't hungry, she was going to have you doing something until you were. "We are waiting on the handyman though. The disposal isn't working right now."

"No problem, and we can eat whatever is easiest for you tonight. Thank you guys again." Bending down, she hugged Aunt Mary again and gave her a kiss on the cheek. "I don't know what I would do without you guys here."

"Family helps family, dear." And that was all Aunt Mary was going to say about it. No thanks needed ever.

"I love you." Before either of them did more than tear up, Kelly changed the subject. "The handyman? Is that who redid the front porch? It looks nice."

"Yes, yes. Bob thought he was going to do it. Took the boards off and then decided it was too much for one old man, like I said." She cut a look at Bob, who decided not to say anything and continued to talk to Hunter. "Thankfully," Mary continued, "the handyman was able to get out here and get it done before you got here."

"Really?" Hunter shouted and jumped up from the table to run out the back door.

"I told him there was a swing set out there." Bob smiled and moved to follow Hunter out the door.

"He will never come inside again." Kelly laughed and moved to the window to see Hunter happily swinging while Uncle Bob looked on.

"Go unpack, and I'll wait right here for the doorbell," Mary said while shooing Kelly from the window. "He'll be fine."

"I know. I'll be in his room for now if you need me."

Wandering down the hall, Kelly opened the door across from her room and was pleased to find an office. Mary really had thought of everything. A small desk sat facing the window with a fancy-looking high-backed office chair, and she could see the entire backyard from there. A tall lamp in the corner would keep her from having to turn on the overhead light to see, and a ceiling fan was a nice addition. The room was painted a darker shade of blue, but it didn't seem to make the room feel smaller.

There was plenty of room left in there for her treadmill since there was no gym here that she knew of, and going for a run would be difficult with Hunter still home for the summer. Mary always knew what worked and what didn't without even trying. Kelly would be glad to get back to work in two weeks in her new office. Thankfully, her legal transcription was work from home, and they had been generous with her time off under the circumstances. She would have a pile of work when she got back to it though. It was going to be rough going back to work after all this time off. Thinking about her emails that she hadn't checked all day, she walked out of the room and closed the door.

Moving on, Kelly checked the room next to hers and saw a twin bed, some toys already set out for Hunter, and a large baseball poster on the wall across from her. Smiling, she walked over and touched it, amazed by the little things Bob and Mary had thought of to help Hunter adjust. She'd also bet money that there was no swing set here before Kelly decided to move in. Kelly heaved Hunter's suitcase on the bed and started to unpack and put away the clothes.

"I didn't pack hangers." Kelly let out a deep sigh. "If this is the worst part, I'm good, right?" Musing to herself, she walked down the hall to see if Mary wanted to go to the store. "Mary, are you interested in running to the—" Seeing a man in the kitchen, Kelly stopped midsentence.

"Kelly, this is Mason, the handyman. Mason, do you remember Kelly?"

"How could I forget?" Drying his hands off, he looked up, and Kelly stared into eyes she hadn't seen in twelve years. Mason Cole.

"Wow! How are you? It's been forever." Not sure what to do with herself, she leaned awkwardly against the wall, taking in this man who had been a teenager when she saw him last. Instead, here was this man with his dark brown hair and muscles she could see through his blue shirt. And those blue eyes... a woman could get lost in those eyes. He hadn't changed much other than getting older, like her she supposed. He was still as handsome as ever.

"How's the set working out?" Mason interrupted Kelly's assessment of him. Oh, that smile, crooked with one dimple on the right cheek. That smile could make women fall all over themselves to get a glimpse of it. Nope, that hadn't changed one bit.

"Hunter is already out there." Mary saved her from having to form an answer. Nothing could have prepared Kelly for seeing this man in her kitchen.

Swallowing down old feelings and trying to move forward, Kelly shifted to look out the window on the back door to see Hunter still outside playing. Taking it in for the first time, she noticed the back deck was only slightly above ground level, just one step up. *I need to get a table and chairs for out here, so I can work and watch Hunter play.* The yard was a fair size, plenty of room for Hunter to run around, and the start of the tree line had been fenced into the yard, giving him a shaded place to play. The swing set was a good size as well, containing two swings, a slide, and monkey bars on one end. Uncle Bob strolled from the deck to the yard, watching Hunter wear himself out. *At least he'll sleep tonight, even after that long nap in the car.*

"What did you need, dear?" Aunt Mary asked.

"Oh, I didn't pack hangers and was wondering where the closest store was?" She focused on Mary, anything to not stare at this too-hot-to-be-here man in the kitchen.

"That would still be Gersham's down on Main Street. I have to head there to order the part for your disposal if you'd like a ride?" Of course, it was Mason who answered. And a ride, really? Lord knew she wanted to go for a ride. Wait, where had that thought come from? How unlike her; must be the nerves.

"I don't want to impose. I can head down there later."

"No imposing at all. Grab your bag and hop in the truck." Interesting how the words he chose said he made the decision, but the tone made it clear it was still her call.

Grabbing her bag, she let Hunter know she would be right back. For all he cared though, he was still enthralled with the swings and slide out back. After hugging Aunt Mary, she walked out to the dark blue Dodge Ram sitting in her driveway. Mason was standing by the truck and opened the door for her. He waited until she had settled before closing it. *What am I supposed to say now? What do I do?* Placing her bag in her lap, she sat still as he climbed in and backed out the driveway. Not much was said on the way to the store.

Staring out the passenger window, she watched the scenery. Everything seemed the same, and yet it all seemed so different at the same time. When they got to the store, they went their separate ways after Mason pointed her in the right direction. She grabbed several packs of hangers and headed toward the checkout. Mason was already standing there putting in an order for whatever part it was he needed.

As she approached, a shiver ran down her spine. Kelly felt like someone was watching her. Looking around, she didn't see anyone else in the store besides Mason and the clerk. Still, she picked up her pace, unable to shake the creepy feeling. She set the hangers on the counter, continuing to look around while waiting for them to finish. *You're losing it. No one is in here, just the empty store getting you creeped out.*

Needing a distraction, she watched the interaction going on at the register. The woman was practically hanging on Mason's every word like she was super interested in garbage disposals. Kelly rolled her eyes. When she looked up again, Mason winked at her. She had been caught. Completely distracted from the creepy feeling, she now had a new one—full-on embarrassment.

Part ordered and hangers paid for, they walked back to the truck again. Mason took the awkward bags of hangers and opened her door for her. While Kelly buckled in, he put the bags in the back seat, then shut her door and got in.

"Didn't like her much, did you?"

Kelly felt the heat creep up her face. He wasn't going to ignore her eye roll. "It wasn't that. More of a disbelief type of thing." *There, that makes me sound less rude for not liking someone I don't even know and positively not jealous.*

"Nope, it's been a while, but you still can't hide anything. It's all over your face," he teased.

Kelly put her hand to her heart and leaned toward Mason, doing an exaggerated impersonation of the busty clerk. "Oh, please tell me more about garbage disposals." She batted her lashes. "I just don't know what I would do without you having come in today, Mason." Kelly laughed and sat back right in the seat.

"Pretty good impression actually. Now you know why I didn't want to go to the store alone." Mason cut her a sly look but laughed as well. After a moment, they both fell into a companionable silence for the rest of the trip. Pulling up, Mason stopped her from opening the door with a hand on her shoulder. "It's good to see you and have you home again, even if it's not under the best of circumstances."

"Thank you. I'm glad to be home. No love lost in the reason for my coming home, so no worries. I'm glad I got to see you."

"If you need anything while you're here, let me give you my number. Your aunt and uncle call when something needs to be done in one of their rentals. Most of your new home has been newly renovated though; they really went all out to make it right for you. Oh, and I'll let Bob know when the part comes in. She said Tuesday, but when I pick it up will depend on when I can get someone to go to the store with me." Mason laughed again.

"I noticed. The porch looks great, and the swing set too. If you let me know when the part is ready, I can run in and pick it up, and then you can avoid the store altogether." Kelly winked at him. "You can just let me know. Let me find a paper, and I'll give you my number." She dug through her bag and came up with a crayon and a receipt. Blushing again at how much of a mess she must seem, she wrote her number down and handed it to him. Saying their goodbyes, she hopped out of the truck and went inside with a smile on her face.

#

Kelly Marie Holstead, he didn't know she would be there today. He could have sworn it was tomorrow that Mary said she would get here. Pulling into his own driveway, he smiled as he remembered Kelly's reaction to Darlene, the clerk at Gersham's. Just like the old Kelly would have done, she let loose with that cute little eye roll. Heading inside, he greeted Shep, his aging yellow lab, with a pat on the head. Shep followed him through the house, waiting to be let outside. Grabbing a beer from the fridge, Mason opened the back door and went out to the deck, Shep in tow.

Checking his phone, he texted Nate, his brother and business partner, about the disposal and the part needed. He pulled Kelly's crayon-written number out of his pocket and plugged it into his phone. *Should I text her now, so she has my number? Is it too soon?*

After deciding to just program the number in and debate it later, his thoughts wandered to the day he had. After a rough morning with two young guys late to work, again, he was frustrated and cranky when he remembered he was supposed to check on Kelly's disposal today. When he pulled up, he was in no mood for small talk with Mary but had resigned himself to it. Then he noticed another car in the driveway.

Kelly apparently hadn't been expecting him. He wasn't entirely expecting her either. He hadn't seen her in almost twelve years, since they were seventeen and about to graduate high school. That summer was some of the best memories he had though. Kelly was his best friend, but when they went to college in different states, they had slowly lost touch. It was one of his biggest regrets. He and Kelly had shared everything—sometimes too much, but he could always tell her anything, and she, him. He knew Kelly had gotten married right after she graduated college, and that was about it.

She still looked as good as ever, a more mature woman and no longer the body of a teenager, but time had been kind to her. Her blonde hair had been pulled back, but it was more than shoulder length and had some highlights. Her body though, she looked like she took care of herself; he could see her defined leg muscles under her shorts. Her curves were more significant than he remembered. She wore no makeup, probably not something she usually did, but no reason to get dolled up for a road trip to move. He liked the no makeup look though, no pretending, nothing to hide.

Just then his phone went off, pulling him out of his thoughts as they headed in the wrong direction. Texting Nate back, he got up, adjusted his pants, and Shep followed him in the door. Nate was going to give him a hard time about seeing Kelly, and about venturing into Gersham's when he knew Darlene would be working. He wasn't kidding; he had taken Kelly as a bit of a buffer. Darlene always shamelessly threw herself at him, but she'd limit it to flirting if there was someone else in the store. The woman never took the hint that he wasn't interested, even though he had tried to let her down gently many times before. Now he just avoided the place when he knew she was working.

Time to make dinner. Pulling out the chicken, he got started on cooking. *Wonder if she still cooks as well as she used to?* What the hell was he doing, thinking about her so much? It had only been a few minutes, and nothing had even happened to make him feel so much about her. She hadn't thrown herself at him like most women, so what was it?

Finishing up dinner, he carried it to the living room. Watching TV would distract his wayward thoughts.

#

He waited in his car with the lights off until Mason had finally left Kelly's house. He had watched her from the back of the store as she searched hangers. He couldn't believe she had been home just a few hours and was already back with Mason. How had that happened? Had to be her meddling aunt. He had been watching the house for the past week waiting for her arrival and would meet her again soon. She was supposed to come back after she finished school, and like a fool, he had expected her to, but no, she went and got married and hadn't come back at all.

He had followed her online for a long time and had made sure she found out about her husband's cheating. Chuckling to himself, he remembered how easy that had been. He had just pretended to be the secretary's doctor and called their house phone looking for the father of the baby. Of course, Kelly had answered. Then he "accidentally" spilled the news of the baby to her. He had gotten her home now. She hadn't been happy in her marriage anyway, so he didn't feel bad. This time, she would be his, and neither Mason nor anything else was going to stand in his way. He carefully put away his phone, excited to have new photos of her on it, and headed home.